HIDDEN HEARTS

SUITOR'S CROSSING: HEARTS COLLIDE

BOOK TWO

HALLIE BENNETT

Searching for more obsessed heroes?
Check out the Mountain Men of
Suitor's Crossing series!

CHAPTER ONE

AVERY MONAGHAN

A piercing ring breaks the silence as I grab my lunch from the small refrigerator in the corner of Design Time's workroom. Ignoring my growling stomach, I punch the blinking green button on the cordless phone hanging at my waist—forcing a professional tone rather than annoyance at my disturbed break.

"Design Time. This is Avery."

"Put me on with Mike." An abrupt male voice comes over the line, and my mouth twists into a frown at his brusque demeanor. No greeting. No *please*. Just a sharp demand meant to intimidate.

Unfortunately for him, I'm used to rude callers and have handled my fair share of pompous asses. "May I ask who's calling?" The baggies containing my sandwich and baby carrots deflate on the counter as I drop them and reach for a pen, ready to write down his information.

"Dominic."

A miniscule crack appears in my composure at the one-word answer. Everyone expects my boss to know who they are—failing to realize that there are a million other Tom, Dick, and Harrys out in the world.

"And who are you with?" I prompt, digging for more information, knowing Mike will want to know before accepting the call. He's forced me to switch back and forth between him and previous callers before to gather pertinent details in pieces, rather than him just taking the call and finding out for himself.

Reason #47 for why I'm itching to quit this job.

"Will you just put Mike on the phone? He'll know who I am." The man's irritation becomes more obvious, and all I can think is *join the club, buddy.*

Because these kinds of calls are the worst.

No one is ever as memorable as they think they are, which flips the conversation into interrogation mode—always a fun switch when dealing with a frustrated stranger on the other end of the line. If I liked pestering people with personal questions, I would've joined the FBI instead of winding up here.

"Well, just in case, what company are you with?"

"I don't have time for this. Are you going to get him or not?" *Shocker.* This guy is rude and arrogant—a winning combination from hell.

"Give me a second." Fed up, I page Mike. "There's a Dominic on the phone. He won't say who he's with, but he's getting upset, so you might want to talk to him."

Mike sighs over the phone. "Fine."

And just like that the line is picked up, and I don't have to handle Mr. Rude Caller anymore. I conjure a mental image of the middle finger to entitled customers everywhere.

"Let me guess." Kristina, a part-time coworker, stops steaming the stack of polos by her side to face me. "Another delightful encounter with a Design Time customer?"

"Something like that. Why do people have to be so rude?" Neither of us have an answer, but we share a look of commiseration before I grab my lunch and book it out of here before something else keeps me from my break.

Lunch is one of the highlights of my day—it ranks right after clocking out at 5 PM every evening.

Sighing, I plop into the driver's side of my car, roll down the windows for the early summer breeze, and start eating, retracing the steps that led me to the rut I'm currently in.

Because I didn't always feel this way. Didn't always have a band around my chest that tightened each time another work day dawned.

When I first walked into Design Time four years ago, I'd been hopeful. Excited. Graduation was coming quickly, I needed a job, and applying for a graphic design position seemed like a good idea.

I figured a custom screen printing and embroidery company could use another designer, considering the demand in our small town—a demand I'd witnessed throughout college, with numerous orders for athletic team apparel, staff shirts, and the like.

After my first interview where Mike outlined the myriad of tasks every employee took on at Design Time, I even accepted the expectation to pitch in with the retail side of the store, since I'd be fresh out of college with no prior professional experience. For the longest time, I've chalked up my frustrations to paying my dues—that if I waited a little longer, I'd be promoted to where I wanted to be.

However, that dream has gotten further and further away as the years have passed, and it's obvious my path will never take that direction, at least not here. Which is why I've been saving for over a year in preparation for leaving Design Time.

Fortunately, living in a small town like Suitor's Crossing and having no social life has allowed me to save a sizable nest egg. All that really holds me back now is figuring out where to go and what to do. After all this time, I'm not even sure I qualify as a graphic designer anymore, or if that's where my passion lies.

After lunch, I return to stitching the logo of a local grain company on a large order of caps when Mike enters the workroom, interrupting my thoughts about the future. I have a terrible habit of daydreaming while working, since it doesn't require much thinking once the embroidery machines are set correctly.

A bad habit considering the number of times my poor fingers have been nicked by needles.

Change can't come soon enough.

"Next time Dominic Stone calls, put him through. He's interested in renting one of my commercial properties," Mike says as he stops beside me, looking over my shoulder to study the pattern created by the needles. His micromanaging has improved over the years, and truthfully, he gives me more leniency than the other embroiderer, Tony, but his hovering still makes me nervous.

"Will do!" I chirp, hoping he returns to his office soon.

Mike has a lot of different business ventures, so I field a fair share of calls about available rentals. A while back, I thought he might include me in his other businesses as an official personal assistant, since a lot of my duties revolve around helping him as CEO. While not my dream job, at least it would have been different enough to keep my interest.

But it's never come up, and if I'm honest, I don't want to get more entrenched here than I already am. It's going to be hard enough to quit. Something I'm still working up the courage to do.

Not because I'm second-guessing my decision, but because I hate letting people down.

Mike gave me a chance after college, and despite my issues with his managing style and the job, there's still a sense of loyalty to him and Design Time. Which makes my choice to leave feel more personal than it should be.

It's just business, I remind myself. *You have to do what's best for you.*

Easier said than done.

CHAPTER TWO

DOMINIC STONE

H anging up the phone, I loosen the tie around my neck and add a meeting with Mike Jones to my calendar along with a note to mention his belligerent assistant. He needs to teach her how to properly handle clients rather than interrogating callers—unless he *wants* to lose potential business opportunities.

Mike and I met last week at a Chamber of Commerce ribbon cutting on Main Street for the official rebranding of Buttercream Dreams and Brewed into one combined bakery and coffee shop called Crossing's Cups & Cakes. Soon Stone Precision will join the chamber now that I finally feel confident enough to lease a physical office space due to our improved financial situation.

It was just my luck that Mike owned a couple of buildings offering a prime location for businesses. A month of searching and a networking opportunity later, I'm hoping this is the right office space for us.

My consulting company has been operating from home through video conferences and emails, but it's finally time for us to have a physical, professional place to meet clients who'd like that option. People trust a company more when they have roots, which I intend to plant here in this small mountain town.

It may sound old-fashioned with the surge of remote business these days, but it's been my dream for so long, I'm not going to give it up now.

However, nothing I've looked at has met my standards.

Suitor's Crossing is a pretty town that offers a lot of opportunity for growth—to become a respected member of the community instead of lost in the sea of people in one of the larger surrounding cities. While the majority of Stone Precision's clients come from Seattle or Everton, our largest lives here. He's the reason I even knew about Suitor's Crossing and decided it was the perfect spot to build my home base.

Tapping the speakerphone button, I call my business partner, Matt, to give him an update about our possible new office space.

"Hey, Dom! What's up?" His cheerful voice rings through the phone, showcasing his perpetual positive outlook—which I need as a blunt realist.

"I thought you'd like to know that I'm meeting someone Thursday about leasing an office space." Turning my attention to the screen in front of me, I exit out of the rental description and move on to answering emails while we talk.

With a few potential clients lined up to help cushion the extra cost of leasing a space, the transition from fully remote to working from an office should be as smooth as possible.

Our business model is simple. I confirm the details and build a solid plan forward, then pass the information to Matt who goes in and presents our suggestions for a business's growth. He's the personality of the company. Smooth-talking and outgoing while I handle most of the research and internal decisions.

"That's awesome, man! I hope this one works out. I'm ready to convert my current office space into that gym I've been wanting."

Of course, that's what concerns him the most.

Matt and I met in college, and through his persistence, we became friends then business partners. But sometimes I wonder how we work so well together since we're completely different.

"And we can start meeting clients in person, in addition to you flying out to see them," I remind him. The travel suits his transient nature compared to my preference for a stable living situation. I like routine. Jetting off to a different city every week doesn't suit me.

"Ha! That, too," he agrees. "Listen, I should go. I'm about to board a flight to Philly for this Hillburg deal. I'll talk to you later!"

"Good luck, and don't forget there's an updated brief in your email." We hang up, and I continue working—almost... *happy*.

An unfamiliar occurrence lately.

And a feeling I won't trust until my life and business are more stable.

"Here's to the future," I mutter, circling the date of my meeting with Mike to emphasize its importance before turning my attention to our next project. Just because things are going well doesn't mean they always will be, so there's no time to slack off.

Stone Precision is my sole focus.

Nothing—*and no one*—will ever change that.

CHAPTER THREE

AVERY

The doorbell goes off, signaling another customer entering the store, and my standard greeting to customers rolls out on autopilot. "Welcome to Design Time! How are you?"

"Fine. I'm here to see Mike."

Whipping my head around at the husky rasp, my narrowed gaze lands on a man in a gray suit—raven hair cropped short, wintry blue eyes staring straight back at me before dropping to his phone, dismissing me with disdainful ease. His nose looks like it's been broken one too many times, and a scar slices across his right eyebrow.

Maybe his abrupt demeanor pissed off the wrong person in order to gain those past injuries.

Not nice.

I remind myself to be charitable, but common courtesy flew out the window about two hours ago after dealing with an upset customer. When the order she placed for her daughter's soccer uniform came back too small, the mom had gone nuclear. Parents had over a month to turn in the team order form. Plenty of time to review the measurements we printed on the forms or come to the store and try on the samples we kept on hand.

This lady did neither.

Just kept harping on the fact that the medium sizing from her daughter's old team uniform fit fine, so clearly something was wrong on our end.

"I understand, ma'am, but these uniforms are probably a different brand from what the other team used. Don't you just hate when sizing differs so greatly between brands? Unfortunately, you'll have to pay for another uniform, but we're happy to offer a 25% discount."

The unhappy mom didn't care for our solution and continued to rant until Mike came out from his office and decided to repurpose the sample size we had for her daughter.

So, yeah... My level of acceptance for rude people is at a big, fat zero.

"Can I get a name?" I ask to annoy the man. It's petty but whatever. He probably thinks I should already know who he is, and truthfully, his voice is familiar. But I'm not going to play along with his little act of superiority.

Usually, it takes a lot to ruffle my feathers because I hate conflict, and I give too many people the benefit of the doubt. Hell, how long have I worked here because I'm too chicken to approach Mike about leaving? How long did I gaslight myself into thinking things would change, that I needed to give Mike time to realize I could do more?

But there's something about *this* man that's gotten under my skin from our very first phone call. And it doesn't help that his presence follows Miss Angry Mom from earlier.

"Dominic Stone."

Be professional. Pasting a fake smile on my face, I force a cheerful, "I'm Avery. I'll let Mike know you're here."

He nods, his head still bent away from me. After telling Mike about his visitor, I return to the front of the store, knowing he'll want to see me chatting and being sociable with waiting clients.

My mind searches for something to say. Which is tough when Dominic is glued to his phone, looking like he doesn't want to be disturbed by a mere peon—not that I *want* to talk to him. But Mike prefers that I settle clients at our conference table then chat to keep them occupied.

Screw that. I don't have the willpower to be the perfect employee today.

"You can sit over there." I point to the long table that sits in our makeshift meeting space. It's really just a larger part of the hallway that separates the work space in the back from the front retail section, but it does the job, even if it is cramped.

Without any other acknowledgment that he heard me, Dominic stomps by.

No *thank you* or anything.

Jerk.

The sweet older shopper I was waiting on when Dominic came in brings her items to the counter to check out, while Mike greets his guest.

Perfect timing.

After thanking the woman for shopping with us, I try walking back to the embroidery machines, but of course, Dominic is sitting with his chair distanced from the conference table, taking up as much space as possible.

Manspreading at its finest.

Geez, we get it—you're a very important man. My eyes roll heavenward, but my annoyance doesn't eclipse the awkwardness bubbling in my gut. I'm not a tiny girl and times like these remind me of that fact.

No one's paying attention to you. There's no need to feel awkward.

But my belly still clenches with nerves. I hate being a nuisance, especially in front of a guy like Dominic who doesn't seem to hesitate about voicing his displeasure.

Releasing a breath of nerves, I stop stalling and continue forward in an attempt to squeeze behind his seat—something these hips and ass were never meant to do.

"Excuse me."

Dominic looks back with a *why are you bothering me?* expression but moves forward as Mike shoots me a sympathizing frown.

My butt drags across the back of Dominic's chair but at least I'm finally through the tight space. Relief pours through me as I scurry back to the embroidery machine, praying another retail customer doesn't come in while Dominic and Mike are meeting.

Today cannot end soon enough.

A message that's hammered home thirty minutes later when the bell goes off again and I run into Mike while hurrying to supervise the front.

"He tracked dirt in." Disgust fills his statement. If there's one thing Mike hates, it's people who walk in without first wiping their shoes off on the little rug by the door. His anal attentiveness serves him well when assessing the quality of our products, but it becomes a bit much at times.

Like now.

Preserving these carpets is one of his top priorities because I'm pretty sure they're original to the store, meaning they're like forty years old. "You'll need to vacuum this whole area." He gestures to the conference room and the path leading to the front door.

Biting my lip to hold back a retort, I nod and pull out the vacuum—another mental check appearing on the "Reasons I Want To Leave" list.

Reason #81: Adhering to my boss's nitpicky commands.

It doesn't surprise me that Dominic didn't have the common courtesy to clean his shoes before traipsing through the store, though how he even got his shoes dirty is beyond me. Dressed in a suit and loafers, he's not exactly prepared for a hike through the surrounding forests.

Then I see the tracks of dirt Mike referenced, and it all makes sense. A couple of crunchy brown leaves—that could've blown inside the store just by opening the door—form a sparse trail to the entrance.

"Good grief..." Plugging the vacuum into a power socket, I slide it across the carpet quickly before winding the cord back up five minutes later.

That's when someone decides to enter the store.

Thank goodness I'm done already because it's impossible trying to listen for the front doorbell while vacuuming. In the past, Mike has scolded me for missing a customer who had entered while I vacuumed, and I don't want a repeat lecture. It's demeaning as hell, and virtually pointless in the grand scheme of things.

This is Suitor's Crossing.

It's highly improbable someone will steal something in the short time it would take me to notice a customer, but in Mike's mind, the town is crawling with would-be thieves waiting for their shot to snag a free item while I vacuum.

Silly, stupid, unreasonable...

Bent over, I can't see the customer yet as I twine the gray cord into a figure eight, but then a deep voice asks, "A bit early to be cleaning up, isn't it?"

Shaking my head at how unlucky I am today, I restrain the snarky response on the tip of my tongue.

Seriously? Why is he back already?

I glance up to catch Dominic's gaze trained on my chest, which has me straightening to my full five feet and four inches with an unmissable blush tinging my cheeks. My blouse is work-appropriate, except for the vee that gapes open anytime I lean forward, so I'm betting he got an eyeful of my plum 40DD bra.

His eyes slowly lift along with the corners of his mouth, my embarrassed stare stopping the thorough examination.

The jerk doesn't even have the decency to look apologetic!

Reason #—what number am I on? Because this list is fucking endless.

CHAPTER FOUR

DOMINIC

The curvy little spitfire's glare could roast me alive.

Avery, that's the name Mike used, and I roll it around in my mind as I fight to get my body back under control. But if she's going to put her breasts on display, I sure as hell am going to take advantage of the view.

I forced myself to ignore her curves earlier, choosing to mess around on my phone rather than gawk at the unexpected beauty before me. Who knew Mike's prickly employee would be so damn alluring?

"Did you forget something?" Her cold words do nothing to make me feel bad about checking her out. If anything, it makes me want to melt that wall of ice she erected.

"Clearly, I forgot to request a view the first time." My eyes drop pointedly to her chest again.

"Excuse me?" Avery crosses her arms, which does the opposite of what she wants and emphasizes her lush tits even more.

"I'm returning Mike's key," I say, rather than repeating myself. The silver metal reflects the overhead lights from its position between my thumb and pointer finger.

"I'll take it." Our hands brush briefly before Avery jerks back, and I grit my teeth at her reaction.

I'm not fucking toxic.

Someone enters the store and without a word, she steps around me to greet them. I hate being ignored, especially when Avery transforms into a different person for the stranger—all sunshine and smiles versus the ice queen.

It shouldn't bother me since I barely know the woman. I've got bigger problems to deal with than a feisty hellcat, but damn if I can resist the challenge she presents. It's been a long while since a woman's captured my interest. I'd almost forgotten how exhilarating the push/pull between a man and a woman could be.

My phone vibrates with a call from Matt—proving that I have no business standing here covertly watching Avery pluck a couple of caps off a rack by the door and offer them to an older gentleman. Dragging my feet towards the door, I grimace when Avery stiffens as I pass by.

Like I'm a fucking pariah who's mere touch will contaminate her.

MATT AND I DECIDED to grab dinner at Daffodil's a few days later to discuss our next steps, since Stone Precision will have roots planted in Suitor's Crossing soon.

After touring the dusty dregs leftover from its previous tenant, Mike and I negotiated the terms of the lease, including him paying for a service to clean the space before we moved in. He apologized for the less-than-pristine shape of the office—blaming a hectic schedule—but it didn't bother me as long as it was taken care of before Stone Precision took over.

The office had the best bones and location of any place I toured, so I could afford to be a little forgiving of its current state.

"Hopefully, you'll be able to get the office in shape for opening by yourself, since I'm leaving for Houston after the lease is signed. Then I have presentations in San Francisco and Atlanta," Matt says, swirling a fry in his cup of garlic aioli before popping it into his mouth.

"I'll be fine. It just needs our desks and computers. Maybe a few chairs."

He laughs like I said something ridiculous. "Yeah... That's all it'll need." His tone throws me off.

"What? You think I'm wrong?"

He shrugs as he takes a bite of his burger. "All I'm saying is we want this to look professional, right? Welcoming. That might take more than a few desks. We probably need to set aside space for a waiting area. Fill it with fancy shit, you know?"

Above the heads of other restaurant-goers, a riot of curls catches my eye. *Avery.* She weaves her way towards an old lady sitting at the bar. With pastel pink hair and glasses attached to a beaded chain, the woman looks to be in her eighties. Is that Avery's grandmother? Great-aunt?

"Fancy shit, huh?" I study Avery as an idea begins to form. "Something an interior designer could set up."

"Now you're catching on."

This is why Matt and I work well together. Sometimes he's able to see the whole picture while I'm stuck nitpicking details.

"I'll head down to Everton Friday or Saturday. Hopefully, I'll have our new designer by then, and we can make headway on what else the office might need." I make a note in my calendar, although I hardly need a reminder to talk to Avery—no matter how hard I've tried, she hasn't been far from my thoughts this week. Not after the way she worked her way under my skin.

While not technically a professional designer, anyone who works at a place called Design Time has to be creative, right? I'd be killing two birds with one stone: decorating the office on a budget and getting to know Avery. Which will either end with this sudden fixation fizzling out or running its course with her in my bed, *and then* fizzling out.

Because I never stay interested in a woman for long. Stone Precision always draws my full attention back to it.

"Sounds like a plan. Are you gonna finish that? I'm starving."

I grunt in exasperation and push my half-eaten burger towards him. Matt would always rather eat than work. He'd actually prefer *anything* else over work, but he's damn good at his job when he has to be, which is why we're still business partners.

I don't tolerate lazy slackers—not in life and certainly not in my business. That's why we vet people before agreeing to take them on as clients. Make sure they're serious and open to advice and the potential for change. I'm not going to work my ass off for someone else to flush it down the drain because they have a terrible work ethic.

Pulling out my cell, I drag my perpetually straying gaze away from Avery to catch up on some emails while I wait for Matt to finish.

"It's rude to be on your phone during dinner," Matt points out.

"We're not on a date, moron."

Matt almost chokes on his food at the comeback. "Yeah, because you haven't been with a woman in over a year. Since what's her name... Lydia, Lisa? No wonder you have no manners. You're out of practice."

I take a gulp of my beer. This is one of Matt's favorite topics: me and women. Because he travels so much, he takes that as an opportunity to also sleep with as many women as possible. He's never understood why I'm not the same way.

It never occurred to him that I've been busy building the company. I don't have time to date, and frankly, it doesn't interest me. *Or it didn't*, I think as I steal another glance at Avery. She's laughing, her face completely open and free of tension—a way she's never been with me the two times we've met.

"I told you we weren't going to discuss this anymore." I don't need Matt meddling in my affairs. Especially now that I'm considering letting someone into my life.

Avery and her companion gather their things to leave after only ordering drinks. It's time to make a move and put my hastily made plan in action.

"I'm ready to go. Here's money for my meal." I throw some cash on the table and leave. Matt's probably going to text me asking why I was in such a hurry, but I'm not about to let him know I'm chasing a woman—a beautiful but icy Avery.

The two women hug goodbye before Avery heads to the crosswalk at the corner. Jogging to the light, I lean around her to press the button for the pedestrian walking signal as if this is a casual run-in rather than me following her outside like a damn stalker.

All casualty flies out the window, though, when pain erupts in my cheek after Avery's arm whacks me in the face. Her short scream rents the air, and she almost trips over her feet in the swift twisting panic of her body. "Who—Dominic? Are you trying to scare me to death? You don't run up behind a woman like that at night!"

"Sorry, I wanted to make sure I made this light." There's not a car in sight, but that doesn't mean I can't use the crosswalk like a good citizen.

Rubbing my jaw to ease the sting of her unexpected assault, I ask, "What was that? Some kind of ninja move?"

"You're lucky I didn't have my katana or else you'd be—" She slices her hand across her neck, and unbidden, a chuckle works its way through my disgruntlement at her theatrics.

"Please tell me you don't really have a katana stashed away at home."

"Let's hope you never find out," she warns, crossing her arms and turning away from me.

Determined not to let her dismiss me, I push. "I saw you at Daffodil's tonight. Who was your friend?"

"None of your business."

"Not up for friendly conversation?"

She doesn't respond.

Is she trying to ignore me now?

Grinning, I continue, "How long have you worked for Mike?"

The light changes and my long strides match her short, stomping ones as we cross the street. I'm not sure she's going to answer when she snaps, "Four years. Why?"

"Like I said, making friendly conversation. Mike gave me a tour of the machines. Intimidating stuff. Did you always want to become an industrial embroiderer?" Maybe if I keep her talking, she'll relax, and I can broach the topic of her helping me decorate the Stone Precision office.

"Hardly. I applied for a graphic design position, but it obviously never materialized." A tinge of bitterness adds an edge to her tone. "Since we're playing Twenty Questions, why did you move to Suitor's Crossing?"

As I suspected, Avery's full potential wasn't being used at Design Time, making my plan seem more tangible.

"How do you know I haven't lived here for years already?" I tease, flattered by the prospect of her asking about me. During my first conversation with Mike, I mentioned how I only moved to town a few months ago. Did he share that with Avery?

When she doesn't confirm my suspicion, I shrug. "For business. Suitor's Crossing has a thriving economy while maintaining its small town appeal. A good fit for what I'm looking for."

"Not gonna lie, I'm surprised you were looking for a small town to settle in. Doesn't seem your type..." A black Nissan comes into view after we turn down a wide alley. It's dark here. The closest light is by the street, not behind the building where her car is parked, and a sense of unease rises in my gut. She must have left it here after work instead of driving the short distance to Daffodil's.

"What's my type?"

"Oh, you know... the stereotypical glass skyscraper at the heart of a bustling city." Her hand waves forward. "This is me. Thanks for stalking me to my car," she quips.

White lights flash with the push of a button as she attempts to slam the door in my face after slipping inside. Instinctively, I stop it with a hand wrapped around the edge.

For some reason, our breaths are heavy, filling the otherwise silent alley. It sounds like we raced to her car rather than walking at a sedate pace.

"What are you doing?" Her voice trembles, but it's not fear I detect. No, it's an obstinate attitude. A grin threatens to break free, and it's an odd sensation. I'm not a masochist. I don't find charm in a woman hating me.

Except for when it comes to Avery, apparently.

Numerous temptations pop into my head as I stare at her features lit by the small overhead car light. *Testing the softness of her cheek. Tasting the plump lower lip she's currently biting.*

But none of those are appropriate.

Not yet anyway.

"Next time, park closer to the light. It's safer," I mutter, releasing my hold on the door before backing off.

I'll bring up the idea of her decorating the office another time—when she's in a better mood. A harsh bark of laughter erupts into the night, probably making me look like a lunatic as Avery drives away.

Fat chance of that happening.

Avery's mood nosedives every time I'm around.

A fact that fucking stings.

CHAPTER FIVE

AVERY

After my unexpected interaction with Dominic, I'm dreading work as I park in the same spot as yesterday. I'm not sure if he and Mike have a meeting today, but my fingers are crossed that they don't.

Because Dominic Stone confuses the hell out of me.

It took forever to fall asleep last night because all I could do was wonder why he seemed so intent on talking to me. And how good he'd looked in his casual henley and jeans. The scent of his cologne tickling my nose. His heat warming my skin even from a distance.

You're ignoring all those pesky feelings, remember?

His overbearing manner should concern me, not send my heartbeat into overdrive.

Shutting the car door, I realize a second too late that everything I need is still inside on the passenger seat.

My phone. Keys. Wallet.

Crap, not again. This is the second time in the past month I've locked myself out of my car. Because I get so stuck in my head thinking about the past or future that the present is completely forgotten.

Last time, the sheriff's department sent a deputy out to unlock my car while I was at a friend's house in Everton. Hoping this county does the same thing, I dial the non-emergency phone number from Design Time's landline after punching my time card.

"Suitor's Crossing PD. How may I help you?"

After explaining my situation, the operator says to call a locksmith before dismissing me. "Dammit." This is all I need. Paying to have my car unlocked because stupid Dominic distracted me.

Breathe.

It's not the end of the world. People lock themselves out of their car all the time. I'll just deal with it on my lunch break.

"Everything okay?" Julie asks, stepping into the tiny storage closet where our time cards and extra inventory are kept. She's a recent high school graduate who works part-time as a retail associate, and the days when she's scheduled are my favorite because that means I'm off the hook for managing both the front and back of the store.

"Yeah, I'll figure it out. The cops can't help me, unfortunately."

"Ugh, that sucks!" Julie squats down to search a bottom shelf of cardboard boxes. "Do you know if we have any more of those Suitor's Crossing Alumni tees? I need a 3XL for a customer up front."

"There are a couple stashed beneath the register. I moved them because so many people came in asking for sizes we were already out of. Sorry I forgot to let you know about the change."

"No worries. I'll check to see what we have left."

After she leaves, I give myself a second to relax before heading back to the embroidery machines and officially starting my work day. Kristina nods in greeting, focused on folding and packing a rush order of embroidered Carhartt jackets that need to go out with today's FedEx run.

The clock above my machine reads 9:09 AM. Only four more hours until lunch.

Time passes slowly without my phone available as a distraction. Once a machine is set for an order, there's not much more for me to do in between runs. Just sit and watch for any random mistakes like skipped stitches or a broken bobbin thread.

It's a boring as hell task without a little reading or social media scroll thrown in every so often.

When 1 PM finally rolls around, I clock out and call a locksmith—who says it's going to be about forty-five minutes because he's handling another job in High Ridge. *Fuck.* Why didn't I call earlier to put myself on his schedule?

Now, I'm stuck starving without the means to buy lunch, and by the time this guy arrives, my break will be nearly over.

"Why me?" I groan and lay back on the sun-drenched sidewalk on the opposite side of the alley where my car is parked, closing my eyes against the brightness.

Maybe I can take a nap, catch up on the sleep I lost because of Dominic—who *did* have a meeting with Mike this morning. Now that he's renting an office space, I don't think I'll ever be free of him.

Suddenly, a shadow dims the sun beaming down on me. "What are you doing?"

Speak of the devil...

Keeping my eyes shut, I wave my hand haphazardly in the air to ward him off. "Resting. You can leave."

Of course, he disregards my edict and sits beside me instead, his leg brushing against mine. I shuffle over the concrete to put some distance between us. Dominic's already caused me enough trouble. I don't need to feel the strength of his sturdy thigh resting along mine, too.

"Resting. On a sidewalk," he drawls. "Ignoring the fact that it's the middle of the work day, don't you have a bed?"

A beleaguered sigh follows his question.

Clearly, Dominic can't tell when he's not wanted. Or he can, and the nuisance just likes annoying me.

"Yes, I have a bed. Unfortunately, I can't get to it at the moment because I locked myself out of my car. I'm waiting for a locksmith." Now that he has the full story, maybe he'll leave me alone to languish from hunger and sun exposure.

"When did he say he'd be here?" After I relay the time, Dominic stands and holds his hand out to help me up. "Follow me. I'm pretty sure I have a wire hanger in my car. We can open it that way."

Pushing his hand aside, I rise on my own. "Have you ever done that before?"

He nods, leading us to his silver sedan parked a few yards down on the intersecting street. A click of a button later has the trunk popping open. "Of course. You think you're the only one to ever lock your keys in a car?" He grabs the hanger before we retrace our steps to my Nissan, and he maneuvers the metal wire through the window.

"You're sure you know what you're doing?" I don't want him accidentally breaking my window or anything. My hand braces against my forehead to block the sun as I cautiously hope this works.

"For the last time, yes... You're incapable of relaxing, aren't you?" He continues moving the hanger around until the lock clicks. "There. Satisfied?" The hanger slides out, and he opens the door with a flourish.

My lips twist into a saccharine smile as I brush him aside. "My knight in shining armor." Placing a knee on the driver's seat, I reach across the console to grab my phone and call the locksmith to let him know he isn't needed anymore.

"Have you eaten lunch yet? A sub from Pickle & Rye sounds good."

He's right. It does.

But I'm not having lunch with Dominic.

My stomach growls in protest.

"Guess that answers my question. Come on." His large palm lands on my lower back and gently pushes me forward. Maybe I should fight him, but what's a sandwich together?

It means nothing.

Absolutely nothing.

CHAPTER SIX

DOMINIC

Pickle & Rye bustles with activity as I hold the door open for Avery. It's a safe, neutral ground for me to bring up the subject of her helping with the interior decorating of the Stone Precision office—a public space where a cool head is required versus giving in to inappropriate urges.

Like kissing the hell out of Avery's pretty pink mouth.

Ever since yesterday, my body's been running a low fever. Work was impossible after getting home, so I went for a late night jog hoping it would clear my head.

Newsflash: it didn't.

Which is how I ended up in the shower fisting my dick while replaying that quiet moment beside Avery's car, thinking about how good her soft curves would feel against my chest.

"How'd you find me?" Avery drops down into a chair across from me after we place our lunch orders. I set the laminated number they gave us at the edge of the table before relaxing into my seat.

"Hard to miss someone laid out on the sidewalk like a sacrifice to the sun gods." Plus, I made an educated guess about where she'd be and parked near the same spot she occupied last night. But I'm not going to share that slightly stalkerish detail with a woman who's already suspicious of my every move.

"I wasn't able to say anything before my meeting with Mike today, but I've been meaning to talk to you about setting up my office."

"What do you mean?"

"My business partner says I have no taste, and he might be right. Someone needs to go with me to pick out furniture, decorations, whatever for the office. I think that someone should be you."

Her brows practically hit her hairline. "Why don't you hire a professional interior decorator?"

"Because I have you." *Or I will.*

She chuckles and grabs a napkin from the dispenser, toying with the paper thin edges. "But I've never done anything like that before. Why would you even think of me?"

Because I want you close.

Because I can't get you out of my head.

"You're not afraid to tell me the truth. No matter how harsh it may be. You also said you wanted to be a graphic designer. I realize this is different, but a creative mind works in any situation."

"Not to sound too mercenary... But if I agree, what's in it for me?"

Satisfaction wells in my gut. *Hook, line, and sinker.* "You'll get free meals and a pass to use your creative skills to the fullest. Something that's not happening over at Design Time."

Her shoulders rise and fall in begrudging agreement. The napkin is in shreds at her fingertips, a pile of white wisps from all her fidgeting.

"When will we shop?"

"Whenever you're free. Weekends, nights." I can tell she's intrigued. This is a good deal with the pros far outweighing the con—the con being me.

More questions follow. Details hashed out. Until a look of resolve settles over Avery's face. "Okay, I'm in." She offers her hand across the table, and we shake on it—a sense of victory running through my veins. "Why does it feel like I just sold my soul to the devil?"

Should've known she'd get one more jab in. Chuckling at the constant sass, I respond in kind. "Because you're overdramatic."

"Am not."

"Are to."

"Easy, children." An older woman sets our plates of sandwiches on the table. "You two remind me of my son and his wife. Always bickering like a pair of squabbling pups but loyal to each other the moment someone else steps in with a disagreeing word. How long have you been together?"

Avery's eyes are almost as wide as the ceramic saucers in front of us, and it'd be hilarious if it wasn't so obvious that the thought of us in a relationship is unfathomable to her.

"Oh... we're not... I don't..."

"It's new. Thanks for this," I gesture to our lunch, "We'll let you know if we need anything else."

The woman jerks back at my abrupt dismissal. But how else was I supposed to save Avery from stuttering through some explanation of how we're not together? How she doesn't even like me?

So sue me if I'd prefer to avoid hearing her less-than-sterling view of me... again.

"You didn't have to be so rude. She was trying to make conversation."

"She didn't have to be so nosy," I say before taking a bite of my ham sandwich.

"Welcome to a small town. Are you sure you're ready to settle down here? Because most people are like her." Avery nods to the lady as she flits from table to table. "Curious. Chatty. Small talk connoisseurs."

"You're not." She winces, and I curse my stupid comment. Our working agreement is barely solidified, yet here I am, fucking it up left and right. "I meant that as a compliment. You don't say more than is necessary to get your point across, and you don't feel the need to fill silences with fluff."

When laughter bubbles up rather than a snarky remark, my muscles release their tension, and I ease back into my seat.

"You may be the only person to view that as a positive. I can't tell you how many times Mike has lectured me about being more outgoing with customers."

"From what I've witnessed, you do alright. Every time I've been in Design Time, you end up helping someone who needs it. Otherwise, they seem fine to browse uninterrupted."

"Explain that to Mike," she says, plucking a tomato off her sandwich and dropping it on the side of her plate, where I promptly snatch it for myself. Avery glances up in surprise then continues, "Business has slowed a little since I started. At least on the retail side. I feel like he thinks if Julie and I engage with customers more, then they'll also spend more. Like it's a graph of correlation."

Avery draws an imaginary line ascending in the air. "But, truthfully, Julie and I aren't the ones who changed. Design

Time's retail section still displays items from years ago—some are literally like a decade old based on the dates on their packaging. Is it any wonder they're not selling? If they weren't popular three or four years ago, they're not going to be now with an added layer of dust. That's metaphorical by the way, because Mike's anal about us dusting everything into a shiny sheen of perfection."

"You're passionate about the subject." This is the longest conversation we've ever had, and I'm glad to hear there's another person out there who warrants her ire besides me. "Have you mentioned this to Mike? Because those are valid points."

"You've met Mike. Does he seem like the type of person to take anyone's advice but his own? You two actually have that in common."

"Yet I've specifically asked for your input and help setting up my company's office."

Avery sighs then a reluctant smile tugs at her mouth. "Fine. You've got me there." An alarm goes off, and she flips her phone over from where it's been resting on the table. "That's my five minute warning. I've got to get back to work."

She stands, and I quickly follow, tossing cash on the tabletop for a tip. "I'll walk you back."

"I suppose if I say you don't have to, you'll disagree, right? It's kind of your M.O."

"You know me so well already. Makes for a strong partnership, don't you agree?"

The afternoon sun temporarily blinds us as we step outside to the sidewalk. Readjusting to the sudden brightness, my footsteps fall into line with Avery's.

"Sure... we're a match made in heaven."

I know she's joking, but if I have my way—and I usually do—it'll be reality soon enough.

CHAPTER SEVEN

AVERY

Julie and I finished setting up for the YMCA-hosted Friday night baseball game a few days after my lunch with Dominic. I'm still not sure what possessed me to say 'yes' to our agreement—*boredom, morbid curiosity?*—but I can admit I'm excited to start. I've been saving inspiration photos to a Pinterest board during my spare time, imagining a finished product as sleek and professional as the offices I've found online.

Even my friends Elsie and Grace are on board with this opportunity, despite the things they've heard from me about Dominic.

"It's the perfect way to practice remaining professional with a tough client," Grace had said, and that's exactly how I plan to approach our arrangement. Besides, it's bound to look good to a future employer, right?

A booming voice comes through the baseball field speakers to announce the teams, interrupting my wayward thoughts. We're selling special t-shirts tonight in order to drum up extra business for Design Time. Usually, I'm excused from these sorts of things since I work regular store hours, but Kristina got sick at the last minute and asked me to fill in.

"We should be set to go," I tell Julie once we test the card reader attached to my phone. She nods, her attention glued to the field where players are taking the field ahead of the first pitch.

Generally, Julie works hard and stays focused, but some of the players are her friends, so people keep stopping by to chat, leaving me to handle most of our customers.

Until there's a lull during the fourth inning.

"I'm going to get a drink. Do you want anything?" I ask. She shakes her head no, freeing me to hurry over to the concessions line before we get busy again.

The queue is so long it wraps around the building that houses concessions on the bottom and the announcers' booth up top. Everyone must have decided now would be a good time to get snacks.

Dammit, why couldn't they wait for the seventh inning stretch like normal baseball fans? All I want is an ice cold lemon shake-up. Is that too much to ask?

Resigning myself to an extended wait, I scroll through my reading app to continue *North and South*. The BBC miniseries popped up on my streaming service a few weeks ago, immediately prompting my obsession with the stoic Mr. Thornton and falling down a rabbit hole of video edits of his character. With my interest piqued, I figured it was time to read the book last Saturday, but it's been slow going.

I've read *Pride & Prejudice*, so this isn't that much different, but the writing is admittedly a slog at some points. Margaret and Mr. Thornton are finally about to meet around the time I'm almost to the front of the line.

And that's when someone decides to cut in front of me.

"Oh, hey! The line starts back there." I point to a dad and his two kids ten feet back before noticing exactly who weaseled their way between me and the lady next to order.

Freaking Dominic is the cutting culprit.

"You!"

"Well, hello to you, too." He smirks, and the scar slashing his eyebrow twitches. "The line moved. You didn't."

"That's because a large oaf chose to block my path forward. You can't just cut because you feel like it." His arrogance is so annoying. He saunters around like he's freaking Simba and owns everything the light touches.

Are you sure you want to work with him?

He shrugs his broad shoulders and grins, showing off a crooked tooth that should *not* be endearing. "I'll make it up to you."

"I don't want you to make it up to me." I huff, tearing my focus away from his mouth. "I want you to follow the rules and leave. What are you even doing here? Rec league baseball doesn't seem your style."

I'm surprised no one has said anything about him cutting. Usually, people are all too eager to punish others for wrongdoing, even for the tiniest perceived thing. And now, when I need the fire and brimstone, everyone's fine with Dominic stepping in.

They probably think we're a couple like that waitress from Pickle & Rye.

My body trembles at the thought. No way would that ever be true. The man is too frustrating for me to ever be romantically interested in him—even if his gruff exterior *is* starting to grow on me.

No, it's not!

"My business partner and I were invited by a client. Matt thought it would be a good idea to socialize and make new friends to grow the business."

At a baseball game? I swear he must work all the time.

"Ever heard of taking a break? This is supposed to be a fun evening. It's not meant to be used for your personal gain." We move with the line, closer to the smell of hot dogs and funnel cakes. My stomach growls at the thought of food since I skipped dinner to come straight here after closing Design Time.

Maybe I'll grab a hot dog to go along with my lemon shake-up.

"Hey, don't blame me. I wouldn't be here except Matt wasn't able to make it tonight, and I couldn't cancel last minute. I would much rather be at home finalizing other clients' contracts. But I understand the importance of becoming part of the Suitor's Crossing community." Dominic glances over at me with a mischievous twinkle in his eyes. "Besides, this *is* fun. I ran into you, didn't I?"

"Are you trying to be charming?" Dominic can be described as a lot of things, but *charming* is definitely not one of them.

"I'm being honest." His voice is gruffer as his jaw tightens, the humorous light fading from his eyes.

Oh, shit. I think I hurt his feelings by laughing at him, which is confusing. Nothing fazes Dominic. He doesn't care what people think of him, and if someone tosses out an insult, he rebounds with matching snark. At least, that's been my experience.

Searching for a way to bring the conversation back to familiar territory, I tease, "Guess I can see why you'd enjoy running into me, though. I'm pretty awesome."

"Humble, too." Dominic releases a low chuckle, and some of the rigidity around his jaw lessens. "Yet I'm the cocky one."

I exhale a sigh of relief. Safe territory again. "You still need to move to the back of the line, though. It's not fair to everyone else who's had to wait their turn."

"Geez, you're like a dog with a bone. Let it go. We're here." He motions to the teenager standing behind the concessions counter.

That was fast considering the snail's pace we were moving before Dominic appeared.

Before I can speak, Dominic orders two coffees, no cream or sugar.

Yes, because buying something that I don't want will make up for things.

Before I can add to the order, the teen disappears only to return a minute later with steaming cups of coffee. Dominic offers a cup to me with a raised brow, and the next person in line pushes forward. Deciding not to make a scene, my shoulders slump, and I get out of their way, following Dominic to an empty space away from the crowd—*hangry*.

Where's a Snickers bar when you need one?

"Was that so hard? And you got a free drink, too. You're welcome."

The coffee is warm in my hand as I contemplate my choices. I could toss the drink in his face, but then he'd probably be horribly burned and scarred for life.

Jail would suck.

Guess that's out.

Maybe I should pour it at his feet. He'd get the point without the injuries.

A brief thought pops into my head of actually drinking the coffee and letting everything go, but I throw that out immediately.

Rational thought isn't driving me at the moment.

Hunger and anger are.

I wanted that sweet lemon shake-up and hot dog, dammit!

Seeing a woman briskly rubbing her arms against a cool summer breeze, the perfect solution presents itself. "Thanks, but no thanks," I say, then hurry over to the woman and hand her my coffee. She's surprised but grateful as she huddles over the steaming cup.

Refusing to check out Dominic's reaction, I head back to Julie and our table without a backward glance, leaving him standing alone—and in awe of my audacity.

That's what I imagine anyway.

"You didn't get anything?" Julie asks when she notices my empty hands.

"Nope." Unwilling to explain what happened, I ignore her confused stare and my growling stomach.

Could this night get any worse?

CHAPTER EIGHT

DOMINIC

My feet stay planted on the sidelines for most of the game after our client has to leave early because of his sick granddaughter. I could leave, too, but I'm waiting for the game to end to find Avery. She's remained behind her worktable ever since she stomped off—making it impossible to talk without an audience surrounding us.

Once the final out is called, I pay no mind to the winning team's celebration. My attention is solely on watching Avery and her helper pack up. They refold messy shirts and hoodies before tossing them into plastic bins, then tear down the table, collapsing the metal legs in on themselves.

Spying my opening, I walk over. "Do you guys need help carrying anything?"

Just as Avery refuses, her assistant agrees with a grateful smile, so I heft a bin into my arms and wait for directions.

"You can take it over to the gray pick up," Avery mutters. "That's Julie's. She'll bring everything back to the store tomorrow."

Nodding, I follow orders until everything is packed away in the truck bed.

"I'm going to meet up with some friends, Ave. I'll see you on Monday!"

Julie runs off, leaving Avery and me alone in the gravel parking lot. There's a line of cars waiting to exit onto the street, though groups of people still linger around the field. Rocks crunch beneath our feet as we start walking.

"Thanks for the help. You can go now." Avery keeps looking straight ahead as if denying my presence beside her will make me disappear.

"Not so fast. We need to talk." I grab her arm and pull her behind a storage shed at the edge of the parking lot. It's high handed and guaranteed to piss her off, but we're not leaving until this is settled.

Caging Avery against the wall, I hold both of her wrists in my hands at her sides.

Her curvy body bucks against me. "Let me go! What do you think you're doing?"

"I'm having a conversation with you."

She scoffs, and I lean more of my weight on hers, so we're chest to chest. If there'd been a note of fear in her gaze or tone, I would've backed off, but the only emotion flying across Avery's face is indignant fury.

"Stop being pissed at me. It was a fucking concessions line. You're really this mad because I cut? I tried making amends, but you gave that away!"

When that woman accepted the coffee from Avery, my emotions had torn in different directions. Amusement because *damn, this girl's a spitfire*. And frustration because *damn, I can't seem to do anything right in front of her*.

An incredulous spark lights up her eyes. "The thing about making amends is that it actually has to be about the other person. Not you deciding what's best because it's what *you'd* want. But that's your whole schtick, isn't it? You're all about doing what *you* want, when *you* want, and expect everyone else to fall in line." An adorable growl rumbles from her throat, and I studiously stuff down the smile that itches to appear.

She's pissed.

I'm pissed.

She's not going to change that by being way too fucking cute for her own good.

"I'm sorry my apology didn't suit you," I concede. "But I'm not going to apologize for who I am. What you view as faults, I see as strengths. No one ever makes progress by sitting around and waiting for it to come to them. I don't waste time fucking around with niceties when I can make a decision and get things done."

"I made a mistake. We can't work together." The words are a punch to the gut.

"You trying to quit on me, firebrand?" More of my weight rests on hers until our faces are inches apart.

Although we're both tense with adrenaline and anger, all I crave is to harness that energy. To claim her against this shed. Because her softness is a damn distraction.

Avery opens her mouth to voice another rejection—*reject me*—when my mouth moves of its own accord to stop her, my tongue slipping between her parted lips, desperate to taste her. Even for a second.

And, for once, she doesn't fight me.

Miracle of miracles.

I angle my head to the side, and Avery moans, stroking my tongue with hers, rising on her tiptoes to increase the pressure of the kiss. Making it harder. More desperate.

Easing away, I study her cloudy eyes—full of confusion and lust—so I take my chance and go back for more. Nipping at her bottom lip. Inhaling each hot breath she releases. Drowning in the sweet heat that is Avery.

Until she snatches her head away. "Stop. We can't do this."

I follow her jawline with my mouth, fixated on the delicate curve. "Why not?"

Freeing her captured wrists from my relaxed grip, she rushes out, "Because I don't even like you." Then all I see is her swinging ponytail as she runs away from me towards her car.

Avery might believe that she doesn't have feelings for me, but her body tells a different story. Our kiss wasn't a one-sided affair. She gave as good as she got for that one blissful moment.

A dam inside me has broken.

A flood of need released from its concrete boundaries.

I won't be able to stand Avery not being mine for much longer, and I'm starting to think this spark between us won't be fizzling out anytime soon either.

CHAPTER NINE

AVERY

It's been a week since the *incident* at the game.

I refuse to acknowledge that Dominic and I *kissed*.

Because, for a moment, it made me forget everything. Why I was angry. Why I shouldn't be kissing him. Why I loathed him. *Or why I thought I did.*

No one's ever kissed me like that. Granted, I haven't been kissed a lot, but nothing's come close. Which freaks me out. I can't let one measly kiss change my whole perspective on a man. That's ridiculous!

"Avery, can you do me a favor?" Mike's question snaps me back to reality.

Swinging around in my chair, I shove thoughts of Dominic out of my head and nod. "Of course."

"Can you head over to the office next to Blushing Brides Boutique? I need you to give it a thorough cleaning. Sweep the floors, dust, that sort of thing. My regular cleaners have another appointment today, and it needs to be done this afternoon. You can go home and change, then spend the rest of your work hours over there."

That's the location for Dominic's new office.

My teeth clench into a grimace masquerading as a smile. I swear the universe is out to get me by throwing me into Dominic's path every chance it has. If I were more of a romantic, I might think the legend of Suitor's Crossing's *heart sparks*—a cute story about soulmates—is at play, but Dominic Stone is absolutely not my *heart spark*, soulmate, or anything resembling a romantic interest.

I. Don't. Like. Him.

"Avery?"

Slamming a palm on the big red STOP button on the embroidery machine, I answer Mike's question. "Sure, I'll leave now." As if I have a choice.

Sometimes it's nice being Mike's *girl Friday* because the work varies, and I feel like a respected member of the team. Other times, like today, I'm reminded that I'm just a glorified secretary/maid.

Reason #22 why I can't wait to quit Design Time and move on to something better.

After picking up the key from Mike and hearing his explanation of where the cleaning supplies are, I go home and change into a pair of black yoga pants and an oversized tee. Throwing my curls into a messy bun, I'm good to go.

I let myself into the office and go straight to the closet where everything is supposed to be stored. Mike was right to have someone come over here before Dominic moved in. This place needs a good cleaning.

Dust motes float in the sunshine, and a few dried paint brushes lay on a tarp in the corner. No one has occupied the space for a while as I try to remember who the last tenant was but come up blank. I hardly shop on Main Street since I'm here so much for work, so I have no idea what kinds of places have been here.

Shrugging it off, I scroll through my phone to the "Dance, Dance" playlist and hit the 'play' button before getting to work.

While some trash litters the floor, the monumental task lies in dusting and scrubbing a ton of flat surfaces because the last occupants left a lot of random counters and shelves. Maybe this was a store at one point?

Either way, hopefully, Mike hired someone to pick these up before Monday. Because I can't see Dominic needing stuff like this.

Which reminds me of our deal.

The one I called off at the baseball game.

"He's not going to let me get away with that," I mutter to myself. And truthfully, as dumb as it may be, the idea of transforming this empty shell into a classy office still gets my blood pumping. My Pinterest board waits to be used—not yet deleted and forgotten.

Sighing, my head falls back on my shoulders as I swipe the back of my hand across my forehead.

That's a problem for future Avery.

Mamma Mia starts playing, and I hum along until someone comes up behind me, their large palms settling on my hips.

Jerking forward, a yelp bursts out as visions of being the subject of a serial killer documentary flash before my eyes.

"Relax, it's me." Dominic's rough voice tickles my ear. His breath warms my skin and a shiver courses down my overheated body.

"Holy shit, Dom." I place a hand over my pounding heart. "You scared the hell out of me! What are you even doing here? This place isn't move-in ready yet."

"Is that why you're here? Cleaning it up for me?" His hands roam from my hips down to my thighs, then higher to beneath my breasts.

I shake my head. "Nope." That came out shakier than I'd hoped. Although it's difficult to stay firm with his broad body behind me, his muscular arms trapping me against the counter.

He needs to stop touching me.

It's messing with my head.

"Mike asked me to, so I'm cleaning it for him. You know, because he's my boss? Your landlord?" The last word is slightly higher-pitched than the rest as he places a kiss below my ear.

"Mmm... That was considerate of him. Sending you my way."

Rallying my defenses, I try one more time to throw him off because I'm not sure how much longer I can resist. My head is screaming at me to move away, but my body has a mind of its own. It likes his attention. "You know I'm a sweaty mess, right? You should move away before you start stinking, too."

His only reaction is to rub his cheek along my neck. Against my better judgment, I tilt my head to give him better access, and the roughness of his beard contrasts with the softness of his light kisses.

I am in major trouble.

"I think you smell good enough to eat, and you look adorable with all these little curls sticking out." He tugs on one of the spirals before letting it spring free. How the heck am I supposed to resist the man when he says things like that?

You don't. That's how.

Giving in, I relax against him. Sink into his firm chest and forget about maintaining my distance.

For now, at least.

"There's my girl," he rumbles in approval.

A hot blush sears my cheeks, my formerly even breaths becoming ragged as we stand together—with me living in the moment and not overthinking whatever's happening between us, and Dominic holding me captive with gentle touches.

The intimacy is interrupted, though, when the back door slams shut.

Quickly, Dominic puts himself between me and the man who walks in.

"Hey, Dom, I thought..." the stranger pauses. Long, windblown waves graze his shoulder while his green eyes study our situation. I'm guessing this is his elusive partner. "Am I interrupting something?" His gaze bounces between us.

"Is there a reason you're here, Matt?" Dominic grits out.

Someone's unhappy by this turn of events.

"Thought I'd stop by while you were here and check the place out. I didn't expect you to have company. Have you been holding out on me?" Matt smiles and tries to get a better glimpse of my hidden form.

Stepping out from behind Dominic, I wave. "Hi, I'm..."

"None of your business," he cuts in. "We can do a walk-through later."

It's like a bucket of cold water has been dumped on my head. For a minute, I forgot what Dominic was really like. *Raging hormones can do that to a girl.* But his reaction to Matt is the dose of reality I need.

He treats his friends and strangers the same—rudely.

I dodge Dominic's restraining hand to walk forward. "I'm Avery." I stress the words, daring Dominic to cut me off again.

"Matt, Dom's partner and best friend."

Matt shakes my hand while I joke, "It's not hard to be best friends when you're the *only* friend." He laughs, and I can see why he's the one who deals with clients. Attractive and charming, I'm sure everyone he meets loves him.

The same can't be said for Dominic, who crosses his arms and glares.

"Uh-oh, I think we angered the beast." Matt leans conspiratorially towards me. I look over at Dominic again. Gone is the gentle, sweet seducer from moments ago. Instead, a tense, angry man stands in his place.

"I think you're right... You should probably do something about it while I get back to work, so I can leave soon. I doubt my boss will approve overtime." I wink then walk back to my original scrubbing position, shooing Dominic aside.

"She's right. She's being paid to be here. Let's get the tour over with." Dominic shoots me a dark look after an extended onceover of my body.

My eyes narrow. Is he implying that the only reason I let him touch me is because otherwise I wouldn't be doing my job? *Jerk.*

Scrubbing the counter harder at the possibility, I let out a frustrated breath. From now on, I refuse to be sucked in... into whatever hell kind of spell he puts me under.

One where my rational thoughts and good judgment fly out the window!

"Hurry up and finish, so you can go home," I tell myself. And that's exactly what I do. Barely acknowledging the guys' farewell when they leave thirty minutes later.

After locking the office doors, I rush back to Design Time to officially clock out then head home. The smell of garlic wafts through the apartment as I let myself in, and I can almost taste the cheesy bread we're having with dinner.

Thank goodness for Elsie. My roommate cooks most of our meals since she gets home earlier than I do, which means I eat better than I ever would if it were up to me alone.

"Hey, how was work?" she asks, stirring a pot of noodles.

"You won't believe what happened." I collapse into a kitchen chair and launch into the story of my afternoon. Who knew it would take such a turn?

"What?" she gasps after I finish. We've both got plates full of pasta and chicken along with crusty garlic bread, and the amount of comfort carbs before me is exactly what I need.

"I know. Imagine how stunned I was."

"He came up behind you and... Wow. I'm surprised you let him." Elsie knows how inexperienced I am with guys because she's in the same boat. We aren't hideous ogres, but we have a hard time putting ourselves out there and have become two hermits who stay safe in our small little worlds.

Work and the apartment.

Plus, she's heard me rant about Dominic for weeks now. My feelings towards him have been on full display since our first encounter over the phone.

"Me, too. It was a stupid and alarming lapse of judgment." I swallowed a twirled bite of spaghetti before adding, "It was pretty easy to follow his lead, though. No awkward indecision like in the past."

"Hmm... But it sucks that it was with him."

"Yep. I'm ready for my actual guy to show up! My mythical *heart spark*."

Elsie raises her glass of wine and clinks it against mine. "Cheers to that, girl. Cheers. To. That."

CHAPTER TEN

AVERY

Dominic texted to let me know he's going to pick me up tomorrow morning for our first shopping excursion. I debated telling him to not bother but stopped myself.

Why ruin an opportunity to spread my creative wings? This could be just what my resume needs to land a new job after leaving Design Time for good. Especially since my current applications keep netting me zero responses.

A job isn't a requirement for me to leave Design Time, since I'm working on saving a sizable nest egg, then quitting once the safety net is in place. But fast tracking my plans by accepting a position elsewhere would be amazing.

With that in mind, I agreed to the time and sent Dominic my address, but if he tried to pick up where we left off, I'd shut him down.

This was a business arrangement only.

The next morning, I wait outside on my porch step for Dominic to show up. It's 7 AM, and I don't want him banging on the door and waking up Elsie. The nearest shopping center is in Everton—almost an hour away—but leaving this early still feels like overkill.

I'm barely awake when his sleek car parks by the curb. The door pops open from the inside, and I accept the unspoken invitation, sinking into the leather seat. Cozy heat wards off the chill of the morning that will soon burn off as the day continues, and my gaze finds the seat warmer button on the dash lit up.

Was it intentional? Or did Dominic accidentally bump the button while turning on his own seat warmer?

"Good morning. This is for you." He hands me a large iced coffee with the Crossing's Cups & Cakes label. The sticker on the side lists hazelnut and butter pecan shots along with cream and sugar.

This is uncharacteristically nice of him. And how does he know my order? Last time he bought me coffee, it was hot and sugar free.

I eye him suspiciously.

"What? The caffeine will wake you up, and don't pretend not to like it. I remember seeing you with one at work." He shifts the car into 'DRIVE' and heads toward the interstate. My brain tries to think back to when he would have seen me with an iced drink from Crossing's Cups & Cakes but quickly gives up.

Too much thinking. Too early.

"Thanks." After taking a drink, I set it back in the cup holder, then lean my head against the window and close my eyes as a talk show plays in the background.

Of course, he listens to talk radio...

"Avery. Time to wake up, firebrand. We're here." Dominic gently shakes my shoulder as the hazy filaments of a dream fade away.

Straightening in my seat, I realize we're parked in front of a shopping mall. Covering a yawn, I ask, "I fell asleep?"

"Yeah, you've been knocked out for the past hour. Missed the entire drive to Everton."

"That's weird. I can't sleep in cars."

"Guess you felt safe," he murmurs as he unbuckles our seat belts and gets out.

I'm pretty sure I was just exhausted, but whatever.

Red block letters hang above the automatic doors of a popular office supplies store as we cross the parking lot and step inside. It's been awhile since I've been to a store like this—not since college. The smell of paper and ink is nice. Nostalgic. Makes me miss the fun of school supplies shopping and checking items off the list.

"You know, you snore a little when you sleep." Dominic bumps his shoulder against mine, a slight grin tugging at the corners of his mouth. If he was anyone else, I'd be embarrassed, but I figure it serves him right after dragging me out of bed so early on a Saturday.

"Good."

He chuckles. "You've got a mean streak."

"Maybe I do, maybe I don't." My thumb and forefinger slide across my lips like I'm zipping away a secret. "So, where do you want to start? Do you have a list?"

"See? This is why I brought you. You know what you're doing."

My eyes roll up to the fluorescent-lighted ceiling. Guess that means there's no list. "Alright, well, I have a general idea for things, but let's write down what you think you need and go from there."

Taking a seat at one of the office displays set up in the back of the store, I remove a notebook and pen from my purse.

Stealing a chair from another office example, Dominic sits by me.

"Do you always carry pen and paper around?"

"It's handy, isn't it?" I write 'Stone Precision Office' across the top of the page. "Sometimes, I use the notes app on my phone, but I like having the old-fashioned option. It makes crossing things off a list more satisfying."

Nodding his head in understanding, he moves on to rattling off items. "We'll need new desktop computers, desks, and chairs. Probably a filing cabinet. There are three offices, one for me, one for Matt, and one that might work for storage. Then there's a conference room and the small lobby slash waiting area for clients."

My pen flies over the page as I scribble down each room then look up at him expectantly, waiting for more details.

"That's all," he says.

"Now, I know why you needed me. Do you have any preferences? Mac or Windows? Do you want your desk to have a lot of drawers for storage or do you prefer a simpler design, no clutter?" As I throw out these questions, Dominic shrugs his shoulders noncommittally.

"I don't really care. As long as it functions, it works for me."

Trying a different tack, I ask, "What about your home? Do you have a particular style there that you want to emulate?"

"Nope. I wouldn't say it has any specific theme."

"You're killing me, smalls!" He's acting like a blank slate when I know he's a man with strong views. Carte blanche sounds amazing in theory, but it also sounds too easy because I'm working with Dominic Stone.

"That's why you're here. I'm just the guy with the credit card. I have no opinions."

We'll see about that...

After pulling up my Pinterest board of inspiration, we start walking through all of the office displays. Today is more of an expedition trip, where we see what's available and at what price before committing to any purchases. Dominic snaps pictures of items we both like for a vision board I plan on creating to help us decide what fits and what doesn't.

It's fun browsing and dreaming of what the Stone Precision office can become. I haven't had the opportunity to exercise this part of myself in a while, and a part of me recognizes that I owe Dominic a bit of gratitude. He didn't have to ask me for help. He could've hired any number of qualified designers.

Heck, Mike probably has a list he could've shared. One that includes Luna Fielding, a Suitor's Crossing legend, despite her young age, because she was the mastermind behind renovating Buttercream Dreams and Brewed into Crossing's Cups & Cakes. The local newspaper did a whole story about her.

Yet Dominic chose me.

I'm grateful for his trust, even if I was suspicious at first.

Four hours later, Dominic and I stare at paint sample cards, trying to decide which color to paint the office walls. After catching me stashing stacks of different colors in my purse, Dominic reprimands me. "That's stealing, you know. Why do you even need that many? We're not painting the walls anything other than a neutral tone."

"I use these for different crafts. Trust me, they come in handy," I explain, stuffing more into my purse pockets.

Dominic looks at me like I'm a crazy craft lady, and I guess I am.

"I need to get you out of here before you're arrested." He locks his hand around my arm and drags me away from the aisle, but not before I pluck a couple of pretty blue sample cards from the end cap. "While there'd be some pleasure in seeing your saintly self behind bars, the risks far outweigh the gains. We don't know who could be in the cell with you."

"Ruffians, thugs?" I quip. He gives me a blank look. "*Tangled*?"

"Never heard of it."

Unfortunately, I'm not shocked. "Have you been living under a rock? It's only one of the best Disney movies ever!"

"No, just working my ass off to get my business off the ground," he grumbles.

Touchy! But I guess he has a point. While I watched Disney movies and lamented my career prospects, Dominic had been out doing whatever he needed to do to make his dreams come true.

An admirable quality.

Once we're settled in his car, my purse overflowing with paint sample cards, Dominic turns to me. "What do you want for lunch? There are a ton of options around here."

"I don't care." He suggests a Mexican restaurant nearby. "Except for that." My face scrunches up in disapproval. I love chips and salsa and yummy margaritas, but I'm in the mood for something lighter.

"So, you do care." Dominic huffs as he starts driving around.

"*I don't care* means you don't know what you want but you know what you *don't* want." It's simple girl math.

"Thanks for clearing that up, but we still need a place to eat."

I point to a place on our right. "That looks good."

"You and sandwiches..." he mutters before parking the car, and we walk inside. It's a cute shop, obviously locally owned. Handmade trinkets stock the front of the store while the rest of the decor is very homey and rustic. The chalkboard menu hangs over a rural scene.

It actually reminds me a lot of Pickle & Rye back in Suitor's Crossing.

Dominic gestures in front of him. "Ladies first."

"You're no gentleman," I taunt but step in front of him and order. After refusing to let me pay for lunch—again—Dominic hands the empty cups to me. "I'll wait here. Go get our drinks and a table. I want Pepsi."

I playfully salute him and click my heels together. "Sir, yes, sir."

"Smart ass." A reluctant smile transforms his stern features, and it's a shame he doesn't smile more.

Why do you care?

Right, I don't.

Chastising my wayward thoughts, I scurry over to the drinks machine, reinforcing the walls I've built up between me and Dominic. We've done so well with keeping things professional. The hours spent with him today weren't filled with our usual tension because he'd been fairly easygoing, which has lulled me into lowering my defenses. A tactical error on my part.

I can't mess up now by fixating on how nice his smile is. *No matter how endearing I find it.*

CHAPTER ELEVEN

DOMINIC

After our browsing trip yesterday, I asked Avery to stop by my place today to start working on her vision board. Photo stacks of furniture, supplies, decorations, and whatever else Avery or I thought we needed rests on top of my dining table, waiting for her to work her magic. It's a bit old-school, but I don't mind.

Whatever works for Avery, works for me.

A knock on the door lets me know she's here, and after showing her in, I motion to the photos. "That's everything from yesterday. I'm going to start lunch. Is mac and cheese alright with you?"

Avery nods and sets down a white poster board and tote bag stuffed with craft supplies. This looks more like an art project to me, but I'll reserve judgment until I see the finished product. Especially since yesterday went surprisingly well. We didn't argue as much, and Avery was actually friendly.

Maybe I'm making headway with her.

And if that's the case, I don't want to fuck it up by dismissing her process, even if I don't understand it.

Avery brings the large stack of pictures to the kitchen counter in front of where I'm boiling the water for noodles.

"Okay, I'm going to sort these by category. I think it'll be easiest to decide what to keep and toss by going through all the desks, chairs, etcetera together," she mumbles, almost as if she's talking to herself, and I take the time to study her while she's otherwise occupied.

Clearly, Avery didn't dress up for me. Oversized gray sweatpants balloon around her legs and have a hole in one pocket, while a plain pink V-neck tee shows fading in some places. The mass of curls crowning her head are pulled back into a bun again.

"Your water's boiling." Avery points to the pot on the stove that's close to overflowing. Shaking myself out of my reverie, I quickly turn down the heat and pour in the noodles. That's all I need—to burn down the house while making a basic boxed meal.

But my eyes can't help being drawn to Avery. Even dressed as casually as possible, she's still all beautiful curves and fiery personality.

A black marker appears as she starts writing labels on neon-colored index cards. "The basics—desk, computer, desk chair, some sort of filing system, lobby chairs, coffee table, wall décor, clock. I think that covers everything for now." She hops up and tapes the cards to the board where STONE PRECISION OFFICE is written across the top in neat block letters.

"Now, it's time to cut some things like the home improvement version of *The Bachelor*!"

"I've never seen that show, but I get the idea."

"First, *Tangled* and now *The Bachelor*? You are a sad, strange little man."

"*Toy Story*. Finally a reference I understand." I feel inordinately proud of that one.

Avery rounds the counter and hugs me unexpectedly. It's brief. Barely a few seconds of her arms wrapped around my waist, but it's enough to send a shot of arousal straight to my dick. My hands rise to keep her there, but common sense weasels to the forefront, and I let her go when she backs off.

Patience.

Something I've never had a problem exercising—*before* Avery.

"You don't know how happy I am to hear that you've at least seen *Toy Story*. It gives me hope that you weren't born a full-grown adult," she jokes—oblivious to the battle raging inside my blood—then shuffles back to her side of the counter to hold up picture after picture for me to veto or approve. If we disagree, she tosses it into a *maybe* pile.

"Food's done. Time for a break," I interrupt, glad to have my body under a semblance of control again.

"Finally." Avery abandons the vision board and props her elbows on the kitchen island where I scoop out her bowl first, then mine. "You put ketchup on your mac and cheese, too?"

"Yep, you want some?" I offer the bottle to her, but she waves it away.

"Heck no. I think it's gross, but my dad likes it that way." She shudders in disgust. "I don't know what's wrong with you guys."

"Nothing wrong with having good taste. Why don't you take a seat? I've got this." I carry our bowls and two bottles of water to the couch where Avery's moved to sit cross-legged. Her mismatched neon bright socks snag my attention, and warmth settles in my chest. It's a simple thing, but her feeling so comfortable does something to me.

I like that she doesn't feel the need to be so proper and polite.

So put-together.

Flipping on the television, I scroll through channels. "The Rockies and Dodgers are playing today. Hopefully, we can pull out a win."

"Who are you rooting for?"

"The Rockies, though I'm not sure why. I've never lived in Colorado. Guess I just have a thing for underdogs."

Avery's fork pauses halfway to her mouth. "I wouldn't have said that about you."

"Maybe you don't know me as well as you think." I stare back at her, a wealth of meaning behind my words.

Breaking the moment with a reluctant smile, she glances at the TV. "Not possible."

Turning away with my own grin, we watch the game and eat in companionable silence, until a few hours later—after my team loses—Avery asks if I have Starz.

"Yeah, why?"

"Because I missed the marathon of *Black Sails* because of you, and I want to catch some of the encore showings while we go through the *maybe* pile. Is that a problem?"

Raising my hands in surrender, I find the series and click on the episode currently playing.

"I recognize this guy."

Excited, Avery whips her head around. "You've seen *Black Sails* before?"

If only she got that excited about me.

"No, but I remember that man. The one who needs a bath. I'm pretty sure he was the cover photo for your *Hot Men* board on Pinterest."

Her eyes widen and a dark red blush pervades her skin. "How did you see that?"

"When we were looking at possible DIY projects yesterday. The boards were right next to each other. So, you're into dirty pirates?"

"Oh my god." Avery throws her head back against the couch and groans. "I wouldn't classify Charles Vane as a dirty pirate. He's a hot, rugged man who manages to make dirt and blood look sexy. The fact that he's a pirate adds to his dangerous appeal. Plus, he's had such a hard life. That stupid chick betrayed him and broke his heart and..."

I cut her off. "You have a lot of feelings for this guy." *Is it possible to be jealous of a fictional TV character?* "But you do realize he doesn't exist, right?"

"Actually, he did exist back in the 18th century. And the actor is real. See?" She scrolls through her phone and shoves the screen at me.

A different man stands there shirtless.

"How many semi-naked guys do you have on your phone?"

Confused, Avery glances at the screen again and mutters an epithet under her breath. "I scrolled too far." Finding the right picture, she shows me the actor dressed in a suit with his hair cut. "And I don't have naked guys saved to my phone. They're all on this board. For... well, just for whenever." She huffs as she puts her phone away and tries to end the conversation by returning her attention to the TV screen.

I mute the show. "Not so fast. Define *whenever*." Curiosity is killing me to know what she's using those pictures for. I wouldn't have thought Miss Perfect would keep what amounted to a secret porn stash stored on her phone.

"Nope. You can unmute now."

"Sorry, firebrand. No can do. I want to know what you're keeping those pictures for. You want me to guess?"

Avery glares at me.

"I'm sure I can already imagine what your perverted mind is concocting. But it's nothing so sordid. Can't a woman appreciate people's attractiveness? Is there something so wrong with that?"

She's definitely not telling me the whole truth, but it's good enough for now.

Because I don't plan on her needing pictures of other men to fulfill her needs for very much longer.

CHAPTER TWELVE

AVERY

E lsie's talking to somebody at our front door, so I pause *Tangled* on my laptop and carefully crawl to the end of my bed, peering around the bedroom door into the living area.

It's Dominic.

Dominic is here.

At my apartment.

Elsie lets him inside, and I scramble backward to avoid being caught spying. When I look up from my nest of blankets, Dominic is at the foot of my bed with a grocery bag in his hand.

"What are you doing here?" I texted him earlier that I wasn't feeling up to working on office plans today. My period started in the middle of the night, which means I woke up with awful cramps and a headache. I've already taken a Midol to relieve some of the symptoms, but the cramps are being uncooperative, hence the need for a feel-good Disney movie.

"I figured we're both having a bad day, so I'd join you. I brought medicine since I wasn't sure what was wrong with you." He holds up the bag.

That's sweet.

"Thanks, but none of that can cure what I have," I say awkwardly. "Since you're here, though, I guess you can stay." I pat the space next to me, wondering what the hell I'm doing.

My bed is twin-sized and wedged between the wall and Elsie's bed because our room is so tiny. It's close quarters, yet here I am inviting Dominic to join me.

A large mountain of a man who will dwarf the itty bitty mattress.

And me.

"There won't be a lot of space, but if you can handle it, so can I."

Kicking off his shoes, he climbs in beside me after setting the bag down. The bed rocks with each movement as he gets situated.

Why did I think this was a good idea again?

"Be careful! I don't want us to fall through. The frame has wheels that don't lock and the mattress is being held up by two by fours."

Dominic shoots me a look of wild disbelief. "Why? Just... why?"

Embarrassment spreads over my cheeks. This is such a bad idea. I hadn't planned to sleep on something so rickety when I bought the frame, but these kinds of frames don't come stationary or with beams to actually hold a bed. A fact the salesman failed to mention to my newly graduated twenty-two year old self years ago.

So I made it work. Kind of.

Dominic mutters inaudibly to himself after I explain the situation. When he finally settles, he props his head on his hand and lays on his side facing me.

Damn, he's big.

My back is pressed against the wall in an effort to put some space between our chests, but it's not exactly working. I still feel his heat. Smell his cologne. Can study the navy flecks in his eyes.

"What do you have that's so incurable?"

Thankful for the distraction from my perusal of his firm body, the opportunity to shock him is too irresistible.

"Mother Nature's gift."

"Oh." Now, *he's* the one blushing. Why is that so adorable? "What are you watching?"

Deciding not to tease him for his reaction about my period, I remind him of the other day when I mentioned *Tangled* and how it prompted a rewatch. "I'll start it over, so you can see it from the beginning. You'll like Flynn."

"You don't—" He tries to stop me from restarting, but I shush him. He's going to watch this movie and enjoy it.

We lay together for the duration of the movie, and I studiously ignore the hormones dancing around my body. Apparently, they've decided that cramping is over and now it's time to morph into lust. If I were by myself, I'd grab my vibrator and let the sweet endorphins of an orgasm make me feel better, but I'm not alone. Elsie's in the living room, and Dominic's practically tangled up with me in bed.

Once the movie ends, Dominic agrees with me about Flynn and admits that the movie wasn't bad.

"See? I told you so." Happy that I created another *Tangled* fan, I close my laptop and fully lay back on my pillow. Which has me looking up at the sharp lines of Dominic's stubbled jaw.

Don't touch. Don't touch.

"What was so bad about your day?" I blurt out. "It's the weekend."

He's silent for a moment then, "One of our clients is switching to a different firm. They said they wanted a company with more experience."

"That sucks. What made them decide to switch?"

"Don't know. I tried convincing them to stay. Reiterated my commitment to working with them, but they wouldn't listen. We can't afford to start losing clients. Not with us finally moving into an office."

Frustration and concern outline his features. This is taking more of a toll on him than I realized because he looks worn out. Dark shadows lie under his eyes from lack of sleep and worry lines crease his forehead.

"I hate how everyone expects you to have a certain amount of experience, but they won't let you acquire it by actually working with you. It's so unfair."

"Agreed." It's a catch-22 that I've also experienced because the same thing happened to me when I graduated college.

All the jobs I was interested in required at least five years of work experience in the field, plus whatever other hoops they wanted me to jump through. It was tough going there for a while. Which is why I was so grateful when I got the job at Design Time. It wasn't exactly what I was looking for, but at least it was in a career path that I wanted to be on.

Or so I thought.

Dominic sighs and rests his head next to mine. We stare at the ceiling, contemplating our situations. Dominic is only a few years older than me, but he seems light years ahead when it comes to our careers. It's surprising that he still has to deal with people not taking him seriously or expecting more from him. I mean, he owns a freaking company! How is that not impressive enough?

Yawning, my lashes flutter shut. "People are dumb."

"And quick to judge."

"Mmmhmm."

He readjusts on top of the covers, removing the laptop from my legs. "Are you falling asleep on me?"

I shake my head but don't open my eyes, "Maybe... A nap sounds nice." There's no way I should sleep with Dominic right next to me, but I don't retract the subtle suggestion. I'm too tired to fight what my body wants—to be cozied up to Dominic's soothing strength.

"I haven't taken a nap in forever," he whispers softly, his breath ghosting over my cheek.

"Then it's a perfect time to start again. Here." I pull out one of the pillows beneath me. "You can use this."

I JERK AWAKE FROM MY dream.

Dominic's arm is wrapped around my waist, spooning me from behind. How in the world we ended up in this position, I have no idea. But somehow it resulted in him invading my dreams.

"You okay?" he sleepily asks.

"Yeah, I'm fine."

"You sure? You jolted out of sleep like you were having a nightmare or something."

Or something.

Like a mind-blowing orgasm from your piratical counterpart.

But no way in hell am I ever telling him that. Because he doesn't belong in my dreams or my bed.

"I'm good," I insist. "But you should go. It's getting late, and Elsie's probably uncomfortable being confined to the living room." Our bedroom is the only way to the bathroom, and while I know she'll walk through if she needs to, I'm not above using her as an excuse to kick Dominic out.

"You're right. I didn't expect to stay this long, anyway. I have some other work to do at home." He removes his arm from my waist and sits up. "I'll check with you tomorrow about possibly going over some more of the office details. See if you're feeling any better."

I nod and scramble out of bed to escort him to the front door. After saying goodbye, I shut it with relief.

"That was interesting," Elsie drawls from her place on the couch. I'm guessing she watched movies all day while I was with Dominic.

"Yeah, sorry about that. We fell asleep."

"Strange... Since you're supposed to hate him."

"I wouldn't say I hate him, but we're not friends. He bothers me too much," I state firmly, unwilling to admit to any other feelings.

"Well, he may have gotten under your skin, but I think *you* want under *him*." Her eyebrows twitch suggestively.

There's no way Elsie could know about my dream, but that doesn't stop a hot flush from rising at how close she is to the truth. Hurrying back to the safety of my bed, I yell at her to shut up.

Elsie just laughs—knowing she hit the nail on the head.

CHAPTER THIRTEEN

AVERY

A few weeks ago, I met up with Louise at Daffodil's, and she asked me to help her set up for a Young Professionals event at the Hearthstone Lodge, a popular mountain resort located just outside of Suitor's Crossing. Louise used to work at Design Time but quit after one too many arguments with Mike, so now, she putters around town pitching in where she can. Like volunteering with the YP group as a mentor and offering to organize their Summer Soiree.

Completing the final centerpiece, I step back to take stock of the room. The walls are lined with giant balloon installations while leafy branches covered in string lights decorate the dozens of tables circling a dance floor. The gorgeous backdrop of mountain peaks adds to the atmospheric glow of LED candles.

The Hearthstone Lodge earns its reputation as a classy venue for weddings, vacations, and business retreats every day of the year—summer or winter—and though I'm partial to its late fall/early winter charm, the current July view isn't too shabby.

"I think we're ready to open the doors. You did a great job!" Louise says before hugging me.

I thank her for the compliment, but she's the one who organized everything. I was just along for the ride.

"If everything's good to go, I'm going to change. See you soon." Exiting the ballroom, I find the elevators and head up to the room I booked for tonight, choosing to treat myself with a mini staycation this weekend rather than driving home when the evening ends.

Elsie is already waiting in the room since I let her in earlier. "Are you ready for this?" She wields a mascara wand like she's my fairy godmother and pats the chair in front of her.

"For the one time I get to dress this fancy? You know it!" My normal routine is pretty basic, and most days I don't even bother with makeup since I'm mostly in the back of Design Time hidden by an embroidery machine.

But tonight is different.

Sitting down in front of the mirror Elsie brought, I let her work her magic. She's talented at hair and make up, spending a lot of time watching YouTube tutorials. I've told her she should look into switching to cosmetology rather than sticking it out at the elementary school, but she keeps saying it's just a hobby.

While Elsie primps and curls, my gaze wanders to the dress hanging on the back of the wardrobe. It's a deep blush with a pretty lace overlay. The hem falls a few inches above my knees, but the neckline is modest enough for a professional event. An empire waist draws attention up to my breasts without being sleazy, and the skirt skims over my round belly. When I first tried it on, I felt like a delicate princess in it, which is saying a lot because I've never used the word 'delicate' to describe myself. Neither has anyone else.

"There. All done." Elsie finishes the final touch and holds up a small mirror.

A cautious smile reflects back at me. It isn't often I'm able to get dressed up, so it's nice seeing myself decked out. "It looks awesome. Thank you!"

She shrugs off the compliment with a wave of her hand before disappearing into the bathroom to get herself ready, too. Twenty minutes later, we return to the main ballroom to find it crowded with people. I expect to see Dominic, and possibly Matt, schmoozing people in order to make up for the client they lost, since not even a recreational baseball game was safe from them working.

While the purpose of YP events is to network—most of their meetings involve some sort of professional development lecture—according to Louise, the Summer Soiree is supposed to be more relaxed and focused on fun rather than business. A miniature summer vacation, so to speak.

"Let's find seats," I say as my eyes search the room for Louise, who's sitting at a table with a couple of empty chairs. *Excellent.* Louise provides the perfect buffer for Elsie and me to keep to ourselves before dinner is served. We're not the most outgoing people, and networking has never been my strong point, which sucks when that's how you get ahead in the world. But Louise has no problem chatting with strangers and diverting attention to herself.

"Lots of attractive men in suits here." Elsie's admiring gaze flits around the ballroom.

"Plan on approaching one?" I tease, knowing full well she wouldn't dare.

Just like me.

Eventually, an emcee asks everyone to take their seats as waiters begin serving dinner. The meal passes quickly with the conversation at our table continuing without much input needed from us, and soon, people are moving to the middle of the floor to dance.

Louise hired a DJ instead of a live band, and he plays an array of songs meant to suit every musical taste. I've seen Dominic deep in discussion a few times at the edges of the ballroom, and while I didn't catch any of the conversations, things weren't going too well judging by the faces of the people he was talking to.

A rising tide of sympathy spills forward. Dominic may be talented at the actual business part of his company but the socializing side appears to be his downfall. Granted, I haven't seen him in action, but from what I've gleaned from past conversations and just being around him, he tends to steamroll over people. Not the best way to attract clients who want to feel like their opinions matter. Which is why his partner Matt is so necessary.

Unable to stop my psychoanalyzing, I watch him drink alone by the bar when a guy who works at the business across the street from Design Time approaches our table. He comes in every once in a while when they need a fresh batch of embroidered polos for new hires.

"Hi, I'm Josh. You may not remember, but I work at Suitor's Lawncare Solutions, and you're at Design Time, right?" I nod and shake his hand. He's a cute guy. Tall with brown eyes and in a fitted navy suit with no tie. "Would you like to dance?"

He offers his hand, and deciding to be brave for once, I spare a glance toward Elsie, who gives me a subtle thumbs up, before letting him lead me to the dance floor as the beginning notes of *At Last* by Etta James drifts through the room's speakers.

I've danced with two men before, and neither of them went well. The first time was at a friend's wedding when my crush asked me to dance. He actually taught lessons on the side, but even though I warned him about my two left feet, he twirled me around like a seasoned pro from *Dancing with the Stars* while I tried to look graceful being thrown across the floor. A monumental failure based on the pictures Elsie took of my terrified face during the momentous occasion.

Suffice to say, nothing ever came from that crush.

The next time was at a school dance my senior year of college. I was paired with a freshman because my roommate and her boyfriend had sort of taken him under their wing. He was sweet but overly eager and desperate to impress me. Which is how I ended up being spun in circles and dangerous dips until dizziness set in.

So, my luck with dancing partners is very, very bad.

Though Josh seems normal so far.

He places one hand on my waist and holds my hand out with the other. We slowly sway back and forth as he explains his job at Suitor's Lawncare Solutions. The physical location houses offices in the back while the front is occupied by lawn equipment, and he handles their accounting. "I didn't know how I'd feel working at a small family business. There are pros and cons, you know?" I don't answer as he continues, "But the moment I started, everything sort of fell into place."

"That's great," I say, absentmindedly looking around the room. Josh keeps talking with very little encouragement from me. All I have to do is smile and laugh at appropriate places, and he goes on and on.

Guess the third time's not a charm after all.

CHAPTER FOURTEEN

DOMINIC

A very's dancing with a man I've never seen before.

They shuffle across the dance floor as he makes her laugh. Her curls are subdued and pulled back on either side of her head, her rosy cheeks glowing beneath the soft lighting. I down more of my whiskey and continue to stare.

I probably look like a stalker, but hell... This guy is dancing with *my* woman.

I haven't kissed Avery since that afternoon she cleaned out the office, and it's been torture. We've spent a considerable amount of time shopping and working out plans for the space, but she's kept it strictly professional. Holding me at a distance except for when her guard was down during her period.

That wall she's erected needs to fall before I throw her over my shoulder and haul her back to my home like a damn caveman.

When the song ends, Avery and the man part ways, allowing me to breathe a little easier. She makes her way to the bar, so I casually ask for another whiskey to look as if I hadn't been about to go Neanderthal on her curvy little ass.

"Hey." Her elbow nudges my side as she asks for the event's signature drink: The Bee's Knees, gin with honey and lemon. Avery's sweet scent drifts over to me, and I inhale deeply. A mix of coconut and vanilla—exotic yet familiar.

I return her greeting and try to tame the hard-on pressing against my zipper. Her pink dress is killing me with every flirty swish against my leg, and despite the modest neckline, her breasts rise slightly over the top. It's sexy and adorable and obliterates all rational thoughts from my brain.

Avery clears her throat, and my gaze lifts to see her features scrunched into a questioning expression.

"I asked if you wanted to dance? You've been alone over here for who knows how long when you should be enjoying tonight. It's not like these things happen very often."

I'm glad they *don't* occur more than a couple times a year. They're a bore when the purpose is fun versus business-related. Frankly, the informative lectures are more my style.

"No, thanks." I'm not much of a dancer and don't feel like embarrassing myself in front of all these people and Avery, but she grabs my hand anyway.

"I'm not taking no for an answer." *Surprise, surprise.* Her stubbornness knows no bounds, yet she says *I'm* the one who railroads people. "Besides, I'm doing you a favor. You need to loosen up."

A fast-paced song from the eighties plays loudly over the speakers. "Come on!" Avery steps side to side as if trying to teach me how to move, but I cross my arms and refuse to wiggle, gyrate, or shake anything to the tune of a Whitney Houston melody.

Pouting, Avery drops the lesson with a mock growl. "Fine, be that way. But don't think that's gonna stop me." Her body undulates more freely, and she shoots a coy look over her shoulder as she twirls in front of me like a pretty fairy straight from *A Midsummer Night's Dream.*

My blood heats at her teasing. Every so often, she inches close enough to touch then jumps out of reach before I can capture her. It's a game, and Avery thinks she's going to win.

She's dead fucking wrong.

CHAPTER FIFTEEN

AVERY

It's fun dancing around Dominic. I'm free to be as bold as I please because it isn't like I'm really into him. Sure, we've kissed. Yeah, I might have ground against him like a cat in heat that day at his empty office. But those are anomalies. Anomalies brought on by dumb hormones.

Because it can't be anything more.

Dominic frustrates me. Brings out my snarky side. And, apparently, doesn't like to dance.

That's three strikes in my book.

Don't forget you plan on ditching Suitor's Crossing for opportunities elsewhere, too. Not that I want to leave town, but it's most likely any new job I get won't be here.

The upbeat song ends and a slower one replaces it. Out of breath, I stop in front of Dominic, prepared for him to stalk off the dance floor after my little show, but instead, he tugs me closer with two large hands clamped around my waist. Immediately, my palms go to his broad shoulders for balance.

"I thought you didn't like dancing. Now you have a change of heart?"

Confusing man!

"This is more my pace," he explains as the knuckles of one hand wander up and down my stomach, each time moving higher then lower as if he can't decide what he wants to touch first.

I try forcing some space between us, but Dominic's hold tightens. "You're too close." My voice comes out breathier than I'd like, revealing my inner turmoil.

We've been doing so well keeping things professional. I figured he'd given up and moved on to some other, more willing woman.

The thought causes a slight pang in my chest, but I shove that down deep. I don't want to feel anything more for Dominic than general friendliness.

That's it. *Period.*

"I'm not close enough."

The rumbled admission has my body swaying forward, attempting to erase the distance between us, despite the warning bells in my head. His mouth hovers right above mine, and I study his five o'clock shadow, remembering the roughness of it against my own cheek.

God, I cannot be turned on by this man.

"I don't like you," I state, reminding myself as well.

"Do you even believe that anymore?"

Not as convincing as I'd hoped it seems. A shaky "It's the truth" bursts free as I tear myself away from his possession before the song ends, retreating to the safety of Louise and Elsie on the sidelines.

Elsie gives me an *I told you so* look but doesn't utter a word.

Good... Because I'm not prepared to defend myself against her, too.

CHAPTER SIXTEEN

DOMINIC

After Avery runs away, I find Matt chatting up a woman at an empty table. Not caring if I'm messing up his plans for the night, my grumpy ass joins them. If I have to suffer an evening alone, he can, too.

Cutting into their conversation, I ask for an update on any progress he's had tonight. The woman clearly expects Matt to tell me off for interrupting, but he gives me the rundown of his conversations until she leaves in a huff.

"You certainly have a way with women," Matt jokes, staring after the woman's back before continuing. It sounds like he made some headway with potential clients, which is an encouraging sign. *At least this party isn't a total bust.* I don't know what I'd do without his people skills. He's invaluable to the company.

"So, you've said." Too bad for him, I don't need to have a way with any woman but Avery.

"If we're done here, I'm going to see if Kyla will give me another shot."

I nod in farewell and decide to search for Avery one last time before calling it quits. She's not in the main ballroom, which leaves the extravagant hall and lobby right outside the double doors. Groups linger out here for fresh air and space rather than the extensive balcony on the other side of the ballroom.

None of the groups harbor Avery, however.

Pausing at the edge of the wide hall, my gaze travels over attendees until I spot Avery exiting the lady's room with a few women on her heels.

Before I'm able to figure out how to approach her, she whips around on the women. Slowing my pace, I sidestep into an alcove, intrigued by the pulse of energy radiating from Avery's stiff body.

Her angered voice reaches me a second later. "That's enough! How dare you judge him, as if you have any right! You might think he's rude or uncouth or whatever, but I don't see how you're much better. Gossiping in the bathroom like a bunch of middle school girls."

Who are they talking about?

Jealousy blossoms at the thought of Avery defending another man so fiercely.

When there isn't a rebuttal to Avery's argument, she cocks her head to the side. "That's what I thought. Leave Dominic alone, and focus on your own issues." The women scatter, uncomfortable with being called out for their catty behavior, and I stand in awe of Avery's defense of me.

My glorious avenging angel.

She may want to deny it, but Avery has feelings for me. I just have to keep poking at that hard shell she's built around herself.

My arm wraps around her waist and spins her deeper into the dark alcove as she marches past. Remembering the last time I surprised Avery and the smack to my face, I sidle to to the left to avoid a possible hit, but almost immediately, she recognizes me, and her body relaxes, realizing it's safe.

As if I'd ever harm her—or let anyone else.

"I heard you just now. That doesn't sound like the actions of someone who hates me."

Avery avoids my gaze. "I would've done that for anyone. They were being mean."

I shrug. It doesn't matter if she'd defend someone else the same way, because tonight? It was for me. No one's ever stood up for me before. Not my few friends. And definitely not my family who basically disowned me the moment I turned eighteen.

"I need to thank you." I lean in and tease the corners of her mouth with my own, brushing them gently back and forth until her lips part with a soft sigh. Her addictive taste floods my senses as my tongue roughly strokes hers, eliciting a sexy moan from her throat.

When we separate for a breath, she whispers, "You're welcome."

"I'm not done yet, firebrand."

Her cloudy eyes widen as my thigh parts her legs and slightly lifts her up so she's at my mercy. Trailing kisses down her neck, my hand slips under this damn enticing dress until it meets lace panties. *Wet* lace panties.

Fuck yes, Avery wants me.

I push the flimsy fabric aside and drag my fingers from slit to clit, groaning at the slick ease of my path. Her breath hitches at the new sensation as I continue petting her pussy.

"A proper thank you requires at least one orgasm, especially when your sweet little cunt is begging for it." I raise my gleaming fingers for a moment, grinning at her squeak of embarrassment. "See, firebrand? You're dripping. Your body can't hide how you feel, Avery." I suck her cream off my fingers and promise that the next time we're alone, I'm drinking straight from the source—burying my face between her thick thighs.

"Dominic..."

I shush her with my mouth, stealing my name from her lips before any of the other guests hear her. I don't give a fuck myself. I want everyone to know she's mine. But Avery wouldn't appreciate being the subject of curious or judgmental looks, and it's my job to protect her. A job I take very seriously.

My movements become rougher as her body tenses, hurtling closer to her climax. Bites of pain string along my arms where her nails dig into my sleeves. Pre-cum coats the tip of my dick, ready to explode, and thank fuck my black slacks will hide the damp spot.

"Come on, baby," I whisper as my thigh grinds harder against her, my fingers circling her clit. "Come for me."

A death grip strangles my biceps, and Avery burrows her face into my neck as a long moan of release vibrates over my skin. The intoxicating scent of her arousal mixes with the perfume I noticed earlier—beckoning me closer. Demanding she stay locked in my arms forever.

But of course, that's impossible.

We're at a public event. Any moment now someone could walk by, glance to the side, and see us.

Tenderly lowering my girl to the ground, I softly murmur a *thank you*, nuzzling her neck as we fight to get our bearings again. After a few minutes, Avery lightly pushes me away, and

I oblige her, expecting an explosion of regret about what happened.

Though, surely, she can't deny this anymore.

Can't deny *us*.

Instead, she mumbles something about helping Louise clean up and escapes our alcove.

I let her go.

I've made my point tonight.

CHAPTER SEVENTEEN

AVERY

I shoot a frantic text to Elsie, praying she hasn't left the lodge yet, as I race to the safety of my hotel room. The party will end soon, and despite what I mumbled to Dominic before running away like my heels were on fire rather than my pussy, Louise doesn't need help with clean-up. Hearthstone Lodge staff will take care of it.

My phone dings with an incoming message. "Please be here. Please be here," I mutter, stabbing the UP elevator button. I need Elsie to explain what the heck is wrong with me. The hottest experience of my life just happened, and was it with my boyfriend? A man who doesn't get under my skin?

Nope.

It was with Dominic Stone.

"Ugh! You're smarter than this." At least I thought I was. I've never actually felt this out of control before. Never been tempted past the point of my strict boundaries. Leave it to one rude and exasperating man to blast through the previously impenetrable walls.

After ripping off my dress and changing into comfy pajamas, I flop onto the queen-sized bed decorated with a million throw pillows. The exposed wooden beams of the ceiling gleam back at me in all their rustic glory.

All my plans for a relaxing staycation are ruined. How can I sink into the huge clawfoot tub and read when my brain is fixated on Dominic and his talented mouth. And hands. And the firmness of his thigh between—

Grabbing a pillow, I shove it over my face and scream.

That's when there's a knock on the door.

Finally! I quickly unlock the door and let Elsie in before returning to my former position on the bed. Elsie sits at the end of the mattress, her phone on speaker so Grace can weigh in on my debacle, too. The three of us became friends in college and have remained close throughout the years. Grace has even mentioned moving back to Suitor's Crossing to get the gang back together.

"What's wrong? Why the urgent SOS?"

Details of the last hour spill out in an avalanche of flustered sentences. "I don't even like him!" My fist pounds into the comforter at my side. "So, why does this keep happening?" I ask, angry at myself for letting things go too far... again.

My stupid body needs to listen to my stupid head instead of doing its own *stupid* thing.

Elsie sighs, her nails picking at a curl of thread protruding from the blanket. Her mouth twists as if holding something in, and the pulse of anticipation heightens the longer she remains quiet.

"Just say it, Els," Grace's voice crackles over the line. "Can't be worse than what Ave's already thinking about herself."

They've obviously discussed my situation when I wasn't around.

"No one likes the girl who keeps denying what's right in front of her face. You like him, so what? Get over it already, and enjoy the ride."

Well, that wasn't sugar coating anything. Propping up on my elbows, I argue, "I can't like him! He's rude. Aggressive. Bullheaded. Why would I be attracted to someone like that?"

"He's also been kind to you," Grace says. "Remember when he came by with a mini pharmacy when you weren't feeling well? Plus, no one else has ever made you feel this way. If that's not worth exploring, I don't know what is. So what if he can be a bit abrupt with people? It's called flaws. Everyone has them, including you."

With that piece of wisdom delivered, Elsie agrees and pats my leg before they both have to go, leaving me to my thoughts.

Maybe they're right.

Maybe I'm judging Dominic too harshly.

But he isn't who I expected when it came to the type of guy I'd end up with. Not who I imagined could be my *heart spark*—but still. Maybe I need to stop overthinking everything, and go with the flow. See how everything shakes out.

Easier said than done.

I've overanalyzed everything in my life. Tried to make the right choices.

Yet look where it's gotten me. A dead end job and a triangle as a support system. One line to Grace and another straight to Elsie because we've become homebound old ladies years before our time. Heck, I act more Louise's age than she does, and how pathetic is that?

My life hasn't exactly been happy since I graduated college.

Maybe it's time to let go of my bubble of safety and see what happens when I take a risk.

CHAPTER EIGHTEEN

DOMINIC

The YP event must've been a turning point in our relationship. Because even though Avery initially denied her feelings, she doesn't refuse my advances anymore. In fact, she's even initiated things a few times.

Life seems to be getting back on track for me as we continue to outfit the office with new furniture and decor. I have Avery, and the company is growing in this new environment. Everything is great which means I'm in for a fall soon.

Avery would tell me to stop being so pessimistic, but I'm a realist and understand how things work in the world. What goes up, always has to come down. Nothing ever grows in a steadily increasing line.

"Pick it up, slacker!" Avery yells at a player on the field. This is a new side to her—the rambunctious heckler—and she's damn good at it. A moment doesn't pass where trash talk isn't flying out of her mouth. She likes to say I'm unfriendly, but my girl has a secret mean streak, and I can only laugh in shock at some of the insults her mind comes up with.

We decided to take a break from work and spent the day in Seattle ambling around the mall—where she'd refused to let me buy her anything—and now we're at a professional baseball game. Avery bought the tickets, mentioning it being *our thing* after the incident at the rec league game. Apparently, surprising me with tickets was the only way she could guarantee I didn't pay for everything while we were together.

My head shakes again at her stubbornness. The few women of my past loved when I spent money on them, in fact they insisted on it. Of course, the one woman I *want* to spoil tries to derail me at every turn.

A trait that's cute and generous, but frustrating when this is officially our first date.

My phone vibrates in my pocket. The screen shows Matt's name, but I ignore the call—something I never would have done before Avery. Guess she's gotten me to relax a little.

The phone goes off again, and my thumb taps the red button. Matt can wait. I'm spending time with my girl.

"You can answer it. You're not missing much here." Avery waves at the green field below where players toss the ball around before the next inning. A protest is on the tip of my tongue when another call comes in. "Answer it. It might be important."

Doubtful, but her tone brooks no argument, so I hit the green circle as I scale the stairs to the concourse, hoping it'll be marginally quieter.

"What?"

"Is that any way to greet your friend?" I don't respond to his comment, just wait to hear the reason for him harassing me on my date with Avery. "Fine. I'm checking to see if you finished the Holbrook report yet. Kessler sent an email."

On a Saturday.

Of course, he did.

Prior to Avery, it wouldn't have bothered me because I'd still be working, but that's changing now that I have someone more important in my life. "Ignore it until Monday. Frankly, I'm surprised you're even checking your email today. That's not like you."

"Yeah, well, maybe your crazy workaholic ass is finally rubbing off on me." He laughs, and a chuckle wells in my chest, too. "Damn, Avery really has done a number on you, huh? Your sense of humor has been found."

"Shut it. We'll talk Monday." With that, the call ends, and I shove the phone back into my pocket. Matt isn't far off. I feel lighter than I have in years, thanks to Avery. Not because she's all rainbows and butterflies—Avery is as grounded as me—but she's got just enough of a rebellious spark inside to trigger my own, brightening my life a little more each time we're together.

"Did something happen?" Avery asks once I return to our seats. She places a hand on my forearm in comfort, and the knots that usually tense my muscles slowly ease, melting away under her touch.

Avery soothes me so effortlessly, yet I guarantee she has no idea the power she wields over me. Covering her smaller hand with mine, I shrug. "Just Matt. He thought about being productive today."

Avery hums in her throat. "Uncharacteristic of him." Cheers blast through the stadium, and she takes that as her cue to move on, leaning back to explain the crazy double play I missed.

"I DON'T KNOW HOW YOU sleep so much." We're on our way back to Suitor's Crossing after the game, and if there's one thing I've learned in traveling with Avery, it's that she almost always dozes off while I drive.

"It's because all you listen to is talk radio. That and the motion of the car are like a straight shot of melatonin."

"Talk radio is informative and interesting. You should try listening more."

Avery scoffs. "Definitely not. As long as you're listening to people debate the merits of different investment accounts or whatever, I'm going to sleep. Especially since your car is the one magical vehicle I can actually do that in."

She goes to pop her earbuds in, preparing for another nap, when I stop her with a hand to her wrist.

"Play it over the speakers." I motion toward the touchscreen on the radio. A few seconds later, her phone is connected to the speakers, and a cacophony of drums and guitars blare through the interior.

"What is this?"

"One of my car playlists. This is *If These Sheets Were the States* by All Time Low."

The trip progresses with her playing different songs and informing me of all I've missed with my talk radio habit. I don't mind, though. I like hearing her voice, and the excitement that washes over her when one of her favorite songs comes on is adorable.

The windows are dark as I park in front of Avery's apartment. A porchlight is on, but that's it.

"Did Elsie go to bed already?"

"Nah, she's gone this weekend. Went home to see her parents."

Our seat belts unbuckle with loud clicks, then I escort her to the front door, wishing she'd invite me in. I'm not going to push because Avery is setting the pace of our relationship now that she's finally agreed to be in one with me, but there's no denying the desire flaring under my skin.

As if she heard my internal thoughts, Avery swings the door open and motions into the shadowy living room. "Do you want to come inside?"

"Is that what you want?" I ask, unsure if this is a nightcap situation or if she craves more like I do.

"I wouldn't have asked otherwise, Dom." Holding her gaze, I step over the threshold and wait for her to lock the door. She doesn't flip the light switch, keeping us in the dark, so I feel more than see her turning to face me.

My heart races at the inquisitive press of her palm to my chest, and the exploratory slide of her lips along my jaw wrests the air from my lungs.

"What are you doing, firebrand?"

"Surrendering," she whispers, and it's a lightning bolt straight to my cock.

CHAPTER NINETEEN

AVERY

Turns out giving into Dominic and my attraction wasn't so difficult after all. Most of the stress I felt about us stemmed from me refusing to accept what was right in front of my face. Go figure.

We still bickered, but it was playful—almost like a form of foreplay.

"You're gonna have to spell it out for me, Avery. What exactly does *surrendering* mean?"

Stroking the back of his neck with my fingertips, I revel in the freedom I've given myself to touch Dominic without reprimand. "It means I'm ready for more."

His swift inhale ends in a growl as he drags my shirt up, *up, up* as if waiting for me to stop the slow rise. When I don't, the green tee continues its journey before halting over my eyes, binding my arms overhead.

"What—" The unexpected move sends a shiver of anticipation down my spine. It's not like I could see much before, but now the dark has shifted. Transformed into an erotic tease.

"I can stop. If this is too much," Dominic says. His low voice filters through the cotton. "I don't want to, but I can."

I believe him. Inherently trust that he'll do whatever I ask. But we've come too far now. This is what I've been craving for weeks.

"Please..." The pleading whimper should embarrass me. I've never imagined myself as the type of woman to beg a man for anything. One, because I've been too reserved in the past to even gather enough courage to do such a thing, but two, because I'm an independent person. If there's something I need, I get it for myself. I don't rely on someone else to give it to me.

But I *need* Dominic to give me everything. Yearn to experience the passion of his full possession. For the tension that's been building between us since our first meeting to finally culminate in an explosive rain of pleasure.

"Don't worry, baby. I've got you."

A sheen of sweat gathers on my body as I freeze, muscles tense in preparation for what he has in store for me.

The large cups of my bra are folded under my heavy breasts, fighting to hold their weight. At least my undergarments are cute with tiny embroidered roses strewn across the serviceable fabric.

"Fuck, you're overflowing my palms, firebrand. So gorgeous." My beaded nipples roll under his thumbs as he molds my breasts in fascination. Or what I guess is fascination since my vision is still obscured.

Which is why the wet heat of his tongue swiping across the pebbled skin of my areolas wrings a sharp cry from my throat, and I unconsciously retreat from the shock. Dominic follows until a wall halts our progress, and he takes advantage of this new placement by sinking deeper into me, the extra soft hills and valleys of my body cushioning his.

"Is this a kink of yours? Pinning me to walls, sheds, counters?"

A wicked chuckle vibrates across my breast before teeth nip and nibble, pulling on a sensitive nipple then releasing it. "Thank yourself for the discovery. Before you, such things didn't interest me. I was a respectable man."

"Debatable," I taunt, arching into his mouth when he switches to my other breast.

There's a burning need inside me. My hips bump into his, begging for relief, but he ignores me, keeping his attention focused on my chest. One hand lowers to divest me of my shorts and panties, leaving me bare to his hungry eyes except for the tee covering my face.

When his fingers slide between my thighs, he hisses at the easy glide my slick arousal provides. Suddenly, Dominic whips the shirt the rest of the way off and hefts me into his arms, my arms and legs naturally clinging to him for security.

Lavishing kisses over his cheek and jaw, a giggle rises in my chest. "You know, I've got a quote that fits our current scenario."

Dominic pauses before carefully letting me slip down his body until I'm flat on my bed. *He remembered the wonky frame situation.* If he'd tossed me in a fervor, I probably would've fallen straight through, slamming the mattress to the floor and breaking the flimsy metal frame.

"Does it have something to do with me being a pirate and you're my booty?"

Another burst of laughter breaks free at the suggestion. "No, but that's a good one. It's less about you being a pirate and more of a vampire..."

Dominic groans and drops his head on my stomach. "Please no."

It's hard to shrug when you're laying down, but somehow I manage. "Suit yourself. Just know you're missing out."

"I'll take your word for it," he rumbles, levering himself up on his elbows to place teasing love bites on my belly and inner thighs.

The heat of his mouth over my pussy evaporates the last of my humor. I don't want to laugh anymore. I want to *come*. Revel in a different kind of release.

"I've wanted to do this since tasting you at the YP event." Dominic's tongue lashes my clit, flicking and nudging before dipping down to lap at my pulsing channel. "I would've fallen to my knees and worshiped this sweet cunt there, but somehow I doubt you would have let me."

"Don't be so sure..." I pant. "I was on edge that night. Another push from you probably would have resulted in that evening ending a lot differently." Like him in my queen-sized hotel bed with enough space to roll around in rather than my measly twin that we were currently making work.

"Hmm..." His beard scrapes over a particularly sensitive spot, the roughness matching the harsh drag of his tongue, and the intensity becomes too much.

My back bows at the onslaught of sparks prickling along my skin as Dominic's thick arms tighten their hold and keep my legs spread.

"Dom!" I cry out, the orgasm rolls into a second deeper one as he draws out my pleasure, devouring me with hungry groans of satisfaction. When I've finally had enough—shoving at his dark head before I freaking pass out—he cleans me up with his mouth then crawls up the bed to rest his head between my breasts.

My hands sink into his hair, caressing him in silent gratitude. "It's going to suck if I have to move." Immediately, it's obvious my unfiltered comment was the wrong thing to say because Dominic stiffens beneath my touch.

He lifts his head and growls, "Why the fuck would you move?"

"Because of a new job. I told you I want to quit Design Time soon. My savings goal is almost met, which means it'll be time for the next step."

"Leaving Suitor's Crossing," he spits out, his fingertips digging into my hip. "Leaving me."

"We wouldn't necessarily need to break up, but it's not like we could have this every night depending on where I am. Though a move isn't guaranteed anyway. That's why I said 'if.'"

"Yeah, but you're not opposed to the idea of uprooting your life here."

"What's to uproot?" I ask. It's been years of being stuck in a rut, and I'm done. Something needs to change before it's too late. He needs to understand that. "Elsie and I are all we have in town. Everyone we used to know from college moved a long time ago. And no matter what, I can't stay at Design Time forever. It's slowly killing me as it is."

"You have me," he says quietly. The anger from earlier transformed into dejection.

Shit. Hugging him closer, I pour all of my feelings for him into the embrace. "I didn't mean to imply you're not important. Obviously, you are, or else tonight never would have happened. *None* of what's occurred between us since the Summer Soiree would have happened. I don't know if you realize this, but I'm not exactly a *hit it and quit it* kind of girl. It takes time for me to warm up to someone."

"An understatement." There's a note of humor in his voice which makes me feel a little better. God, why couldn't I keep my mouth shut? Everything was perfect before my pleasure-addled brain decided to blurt out potential problems.

"We're not going to figure anything out tonight, but why don't I start pleading my case, hmm?"

"What do you—Oh. Oh!"

A condom appears from his pocket, and that's when I realize Dominic is still fully dressed, while my bra remains rucked up underneath my breasts. The thin latex swiftly covers his dick before he notches the mushroom head at my entrance.

"Shall I start with my opening statement?" The savage thrust of his hips punctuates the question as his cock burrows deep.

"That's... quite... an opening statement." My breathless voice causes a knowing smirk to tip the side of his mouth then there's no more talking. Barely enough oxygen between us to breathe as Dominic sets a punishing pace.

You won't leave Suitor's Crossing.
You won't leave me.
I won't fucking allow it.

He doesn't say the words aloud, but I feel them. From the determination gleaming in his eyes. The possession outlining each ravaging plunge.

And, for once, his blunt aggression doesn't rub me the wrong way.

It does the *exact* opposite.

CHAPTER TWENTY

DOMINIC

"**H**ey, baby. I've been thinking about our problem." Dropping a kiss to Avery's forehead after she steps inside Stone Precision, I offer her a blindfold. It's been four days since she dropped the bomb of her potential move, and aside from that, I've never been happier.

Lunch dates. Sleepovers at my place since her roommate returned. Disney movie marathons. It's all so normal. Wholesome. And I don't plan on losing it anytime soon, which means figuring out a solution to Avery's job problem.

She didn't ask me to, but when has that ever stopped me from doing what I thought was right? What I thought would be in my girl's best interest?

"Um, *our* problem?" She eyes the blindfold warily. "What's this for?"

"You'll see. Just trust me. I don't want to spoil the surprise."

Avery hesitates then puts the silky mask over her eyes before I guide her to the first part of the plan I've been working on every spare moment I've had this week.

"Alright, so I know you're saving for a big move in your life. To start fresh."

"Yeah..."

"And it occurred to me that there's an opportunity for you here in Suitor's Crossing. You don't need to move." I untie the blindfold to reveal a desk with her name on it. Instead of using the extra space as storage, I converted it to an office for Avery.

Her gaze bounces between me and the neat desktop waiting for her to sit down and set up shop. "What is this?"

"Your new office." I release the breath burning a hole in my lungs and explain, "For your interior decorating business."

"What are you talking about? I don't know anything about interior decorating." She tries backing through the office door, but I stop her with a hand to her wrist.

"Of course you do. You designed this whole place. And I've already lined up your first client—my friend Todd, the guy who gave me *my* first shot. He's part of the reason I chose this town to settle in, and he's agreed to give you a chance with a small rental that needs staging."

"Are you serious?" If she were a cartoon character, Avery's eyes would be popping out in surprise, question marks floating above her head. But I knew it'd be an uphill battle convincing her that this was a risk worth taking. "Does he realize that other than you I've never done anything like this before? And a home rental is different from a commercial space."

"See? You already have a basic understanding of things." She laughs at my optimism, and frankly, I'd laugh, too, because I've never once been described that way. I'm a glass half-empty kind of guy. Except when it comes to Avery. She makes me believe that good things can happen. Hell, I even visited the famous Suitor's Crossing bridge hoping some of its *heart sparks* magic would rub off on me.

If that's not the actions of a changed man, I don't know what is.

So, I've got to believe that I've had an effect on Avery, too. That she sees what I witnessed the entire time we worked together—a smart and capable woman.

"Todd knows how much experience you have, and he's willing to take a chance, especially since he likes what you did with this office space." *And the cherry on top.* "He's even arranged for a special mentorship opportunity with Luna Fielding. She's a popular person around here and has managed projects for him and some of the other local businesses."

"I've heard of Luna." Avery bites her lip, swaying closer to me as she surveys the room again. This time with an open mind, I hope. "It would be really cool to learn from her."

"So, quit across the street and do it. Let's run our businesses together." I point to my office across the hall.

"Really? Just like that?"

"Just like that."

She walks around the desk, tests the ergonomic chair. "This seems too easy. Can I really do this?"

"Don't you deserve the chance to find out? You have your nest egg, but trust me, you don't have anything to worry about, Ave. I believe in you. I will be with you one hundred percent of the way. I mean I fucking love you, so that kind of comes with the territory."

"What did you say?" Avery puts the nameplate down and turns to me, her brow wrinkled.

"I believe in you. There's nothing to worry about."

"No, not that part. You said you love me. You've never said that before."

I pause, rewinding in my mind. I didn't even realize I'd said that, but it's true. I've loved Avery for a while now. "Yeah, I love you. I'm in love with you. I can't pinpoint an exact moment when it happened; it just did."

"You love me," she repeats softly.

"More than anything. Even more than this company I've worked years to build."

Her reticence shoots an arrow straight for my heart—and not the cute Cupid kind. I don't need Avery to say she loves me yet. She probably thinks it's too soon. But her next words could crush me nonetheless. What if I've gone too far?

First, the office, then announcing my love. What if it's too overwhelming while she works to figure out her next steps?

Avery stands there thinking for another second, my beating heart in her hands, before a huge smile lights up her face. "I love you, too, Dominic. Despite denying my feelings for the longest time. But there's no more hiding it. For either of us."

"Say it again," I order as my hand circles the back of her neck and drags her closer for a kiss—that previously dangerous arrow veering off to stab some other poor sucker.

"I love you, Dominic Stone."

"Damn, right, firebrand."

Then I claim Avery's mouth for my own. Happy and hopeful for our future.

EPILOGUE

AVERY

THREE MONTHS LATER

Dominic's proven to be a very sweet boyfriend—encouraging, reliable, my number one cheerleader. It's annoying how badly I stressed myself out by refusing to give into my feelings for him until the tension between us finally snapped.

He waited for me outside Design Time after my meeting with Mike to give my two weeks' notice. Helped me file the paperwork to register my new business: Avery's Signature Design. True to his word, he's been with me every step of the way with emotional and practical support.

Dumping my purse on the desk, my eye catches on something odd. "Hey, Dom," I call out, and he pokes his head in the door.

"What's up?"

"This thing doesn't have my last name anymore." I show him the nameplate. Where it used to say *Monaghan*, there's a blank space.

"Oh, I can explain that... You see, there was a mistake, and we have to redo it."

"Redo it? There wasn't... oh my gosh!" Dominic gets down on one knee in front of me and pulls a ring out of his jacket pocket. Matt's in the background grinning like a loon with a phone held up to capture the moment.

"Avery Ella Monaghan. You are the best thing to ever enter my life, my *heart spark*, and I'd be lost without you. You took a grumpy, *rude* man and called him your own." A watery laugh escapes at his speech. "I am madly and irrevocably in love with you, firebrand. Will you please do me the honor of marrying me?"

Tears stream down my cheeks. I never thought this moment would happen to me—not with how much of a hermit I'd become in the past few years, hiding myself away from the world—yet here it is. The perfect proposal from my beautifully flawed man.

"Yes! I will!"

He jumps to his feet and places the ring on my finger before dipping me back for a kiss. Matt's cheering in the background has me smiling into Dominic's mouth.

This is the best day ever, and yet, I truly believe the best is still to come.

Continue reading for a sneak peek into the next book in the *Hearts Collide* series, *Wild Hearts*, featuring Avery's friend Grace!

CHAPTER ONE

GRACE THOMPSON

An exploding pop goes off as my car jerks to the left, and immediately, I throw my arm up to block Shadow from being thrown forward. Trying not to panic, I carefully guide us to the shoulder of the two-lane highway heading into Suitor's Crossing and pray we're not far from civilization. My phone's navigation system said it would only be another ten minutes before I reached my friend Elsie's apartment, but that's if I were driving.

Walking is a whole other story.

After getting out to investigate what went wrong, it doesn't take a car expert to see that one of my rear tires blew. "Great," I mutter, glancing up and down the empty road. All I see is a forest of trees—a sight I admired five minutes ago as a Kansas plains native. A quick Google search shows that we're about a mile away from a mechanic's shop called Dusty's

"That's doable, right?"

My dog just wags his tail. Shadow and I've been cooped up in the car for hours. It'll be good to stretch our legs, even if I'm not exactly dressed for a short hike.

"Come on, boy! Looks like our adventure starts now." Shadow jumps out of the front seat and waits as I grab my purse from the console and lock the car. "You really are a good dog, you know that?"

Shadow tilts his head as if to say, "I know, Mom!"

Laughing at his sass, we begin our trek down the road. Like travelers of old, we'll arrive at our new home on foot, something I try to consider a good omen.

Suitor's Crossing is a fresh start for me after a hellish couple of years stuck at a dead-end job and living with my dramatic family. Honestly, I feared ever escaping the hole I found myself in until Avery mentioned a job opening at a local business where she knew the owner, and things kind of fell into place from there.

I packed my meager belongings in the car, then Shadow and I hit the road a day after my two weeks' notice ended. Now, we're finally here... *sort of.* Majestic pines guide our path on the gravel shoulder of the highway, camouflaging any sign of an actual town within its green depths.

At least the weather's nice or else I'd be dying in my cute but warm outfit. In an attempt to dress the way I've always wanted to, instead of how people think a curvy girl like me *should*, I'm in high-waisted skinny jeans with an oversized red and black plaid shirt over a tucked-in tank. Aside from the plaid shirt, everything conforms to my curves, and as someone who never considered tucking her shirts in due to the threat of a muffin top, I'm proud to say I actually feel pretty. Rustic. Lumberjack chic.

Which means I should blend right into the mountain town of Suitor's Crossing. Maybe even catch a mountain man for myself.

One step at a time.

But I can't help getting excited at the thought of finally having the time and mental capacity to fall in love. The toll life's taken over the past few years has drained me of any sort of energy to maintain a relationship, so it's hard not to feel giddy at the prospect of being in a better mental space. One that could result in a loving relationship.

According to Avery, Suitor's Crossing is known for bringing couples together, too. There's an old landmark bridge the town's named after, where couples went "sparkin'" or what we'd consider "dating" these days, and *heart sparks* are a hallmark of the town.

Love at first sight.

It sounds so romantic and easy.

What I wouldn't give to meet a man, *know* he's the one, and for him to feel the same about me. We could skip all the messy middle parts of second-guessing if it's right or not.

Thirty minutes pass before Shadow and I find an old garage with peeling paint on the sides. Its name matches the one on my phone, but that's the only point in its favor.

"Do you think they're open?" Vehicles litter the front gravel area, but I don't see any actual people or an OPEN sign. However, since this is the first sign of civilization we've seen, I hope for the best and approach the front entrance.

"Well, the lights are on. That's promising," I say to Shadow as I push on the door.

A little bell rings overhead, alerting whoever's working that I'm here. The pounding of loud bass reverberates from the back of the rundown waiting room. How anyone is supposed to hear that bell is a mystery to me, but I wait at the front counter anyway while Shadow explores the small space.

Looking for any dangers, I suppose. *Or just being a curious dog.* But I prefer to think the latter. Shadow is a naturally protective German Shepherd, plus he was military-trained, though it's been years since he was in service. It took forever for me to get approved as his owner, but the mountain of paperwork and interviews was worth it. He makes me feel safe, which calms my anxious heart and mind.

Dust floats in the air, and a light film of it coats everything in the room. It's clear no one's cleaned in a while. Who owns this place?

Some old man who's had it in his family for generations and doesn't care about upkeep when there are cars to focus on?

It was probably a super cute shop back in its prime. The decorations and furniture look to be original, only needing some TLC to bring them back to life again. *I bet his wife took care of that before she died.* As my mind starts spinning a tragic tale of the poor owner's life, a younger man emerges from a back door.

He's definitely not the sweet old-timer I was expecting.

"Shadow." Immediately, he comes to stand by my side, attuned to the wariness in my voice. I know it's not right to judge a book by its cover, but I'm a woman alone in a practically deserted building with a man who looks like he just stepped out of an episode of *Sons of Anarchy*.

A girl can never be too careful.

He studies Shadow before asking, "Can I help you?"

His gravelly voice perfectly matches my idea of him smoking and drinking on a daily basis. Habits I would normally not find attractive in a man, but paired with his voice and rugged appearance, they suddenly seem extremely sexy.

What the hell? First, you're worried he might be dangerous and now you think he's hot?

"Um... one of my car's tires exploded a little ways up the road. I was hoping someone could tow it and replace the tire?" At least my voice doesn't reveal my inner turmoil. I sound completely normal.

"Did you walk here?" His dark gaze drinks me in from head to toe and a grim line forms on his mouth. Does he think I'm too fat to walk a freaking mile? The burgeoning attraction in my belly dampens at the possibility. Of course, he'd judge me.

You judged him first!

However true that may be, it still stings to learn parts of my past might follow me here, too. Like men not giving me a second glance.

Oh sure, I wasn't in a place to accept an offer for a date or anything, but the truth was no one ever asked. Ever tested my resolve to stay single amongst the terrible job and even worse family.

Seems my outfit isn't as cute as I thought.

"It wasn't too bad. It's pretty nice out for fall." I shrug, determined to remain composed, despite the insecurity wrestling around in my gut. "So, are you Dusty?"

The man gathers some papers for a clipboard and snickers. "No, definitely not. Dusty owned this place long before it came into my possession, but his name stuck. I'm Wes." He hands the clipboard over for me to fill out.

"Grace, and this is Shadow." I point down with my pen. Shadow must have deemed Wes safe enough since he's sitting patiently by my side with no raised hackles in sight.

Wes nods and waits for me to finish completing the forms before taking my car key. "Sit tight, and we'll get you fixed up. It shouldn't take too long."

"Thanks!" I smile in relief as he disappears back into what I assume is the garage. Taking a seat by the window, I sigh ruefully. "Sorry, about the minor freak out, boy."

Shadow rests his head on my knee for pets as if to say it's okay. But it really had been a shock to see Wes in the place of old man Dusty. His rugged appearance screamed *I could break you if I want to*. Not that he gave off any of those vibes in our conversation.

But at first glance? *Geez!*

His sleeves had been rolled up to reveal a myriad of tattoos lining his skin. No color, just black ink. Which matched his shoulder-length black hair and beard. Honestly, I couldn't tell if he was twenty-five or forty underneath everything, but his eyes hinted at youth. Dark brown with only a hint of beginning laugh lines.

Although, he didn't strike me as the kind of guy that laughed a lot. Maybe they were the start of glaring lines. Can you get eye wrinkles from giving people an intimidating *don't mess with me* look?

"This mountain air might be making me a little crazy," I mutter because I can't stop thinking about Wes and the kind of man I imagine he is.

Texting Elsie and Avery about my situation, they offer to pick me up so I don't have to hang out here. Probably should've texted them the moment my car rattled to the side of the road, but the exercise was good for me and Shadow. And now they can give me a brief tour of the town before I need to pick up my fixed car.

And I can fill my head with something other than the dark Charlie Hunnam look-alike.

Find the rest of Wes and Grace's story in book three of the *Hearts Collide* series, *Wild Hearts*!

THANKS FOR READING & DON'T FORGET TO RATE/ REVIEW!

Please consider leaving a rating/review. Ratings & reviews are the #1 way to support an indie author like me.
The more reviews, the more my books are shown to other potential readers!
And they serve as guides to readers on whether or not to take a chance on an indie author.
I appreciate your support!
XO, Hallie

ABOUT THE AUTHOR

Hallie prefers steamy, insta-love stories where curvy girls are claimed by filthy-talking heroes. And when she ran out of reading material, she decided to write her own stories. If you want a quick, hot read, she's your girl!